A PERFECT EVIL

Alex Kava dedicated herself to writing in 1996, having had a successful career in PR and advertising. Praised by critics and fans alike, Alex Kava's Maggie O'Dell novels have all been *New York Times* bestsellers, as well as appearing on bestseller lists around the world.

Maggie O'Dell novels by Alex Kava:

SPLIT SECOND
THE SOUL CATCHER
AT THE STROKE OF MADNESS
A NECESSARY EVIL

ALEX KAVA

A PERFECT EVIL

All the characters in this book have no existence outside the imagination of the author, and have no relation whatsoever to anyone bearing the same name or names. They are not even distantly inspired by any individual known or unknown to the author, and all the incidents are pure invention.

First published in Great Britain 2000
This abridged edition 2008
Black Star Crime
Eton House, 18-24 Paradise Road, Richmond, Surrey TW9 1SR

ISBN: 978 1 848 45004 2

Set in Times Roman 9¾ on 10 pt.
081-0908-63210

Printed and bound in Spain
by Litografia Rosés S.A., Barcelona

In loving memory of Robert (Bob) Shoemaker
(1922–1998)
whose perfect good continues to inspire.

Nebraska State Penitentiary, Lincoln, Nebraska
Wednesday, July 17

"Bless me, Father, for I have sinned." Ronald Jeffreys' raspy monotone made the phrase a challenge rather than a confession.

Father Stephen Francis stared at Jeffreys' hands, mesmerized by the large knuckles and stubby fingers, nails bitten to the quick. The fingers twisted—no, strangled—the corner of his blue government-issue shirt. The old priest imagined those same fingers twisting and choking the life out of little Bobby Wilson.

"Is that how we start?"

"That's fine," Father Francis answered quickly.

His sweaty palms stuck to the leather Bible. The prison's death-watch chamber didn't have enough air for both men.

"What's next?" Jeffreys asked.

Father Francis couldn't think, not with Jeffreys' unflinching stare. Not with the noise of the crowd outside, down below in the parking lot. The chants grew louder with the approach of midnight and the full effect of alcohol. It was a raucous celebration, a morbid excuse for a party. "Fry, Jeffreys, fry!" over and over again.

"What's next?" Jeffreys repeated.

Yes, what came next? Father Francis' mind was completely blank. Fifty years of hearing confessions, and his mind was blank.

"Your sins," he blurted out. "Tell me your sins. Those sins for which you are truly sorry."

Jeffreys hesitated but only for a moment. "I killed Bobby Wilson. I put my hands…my fingers…around his throat. At first he made a sputtering noise, a sort of gagging, and then there was no noise." His voice was hushed and restrained, almost clinical—a well-rehearsed speech.

"He kicked just a little. A jerk, really. I think he knew he was going to die. He didn't fight much. He didn't even fight when I was fucking him." He stopped, checking Father Francis' face, looking for shock and smiling when he found it.

"I waited until he was dead before I cut him. He didn't feel a thing. So I cut him again and again and again. Then, I fucked him one last time."

"I've already confessed once before," Jeffreys continued. "Right after it happened, but the priest… Let's just say he was a little surprised. Now I'm confessing to God, you understand? I'm confessing that I killed Bobby Wilson. But I didn't kill those two other boys. Do you hear me?" His voice rose. "1 didn't kill the Harper or the Paltrow kid. But then, God already knows that. Right, Father?"

"God does know the truth," Father Francis said, trying to stare into the cold blue eyes but flinching and quickly looking away again. What if his own guilt should somehow reveal itself?

"They think I'm some serial killer who murders little boys," Jeffreys spat through clenched teeth. "I killed Bobby Wilson. Maybe I even deserve to die for that. But God knows I didn't kill those other boys. Somewhere out there, Father, there's still a monster. And he's even more hideous than me."

Metal clanked against metal down the hall. Were they coming to take Jeffreys away? It seemed too soon.

"Are you sorry for your sins?" Father Francis whispered.

Yes, there were footsteps coming down the hall, coming toward them. It was time. Jeffreys sat listening to the click-clack of heels, getting closer and closer.

"Are you sorry for your sins?" Father Francis repeated.

Jeffreys stood up. The locks grunted open, echoing against the concrete walls. Square-shouldered guards clogged the doorway.

"It's time," one of them said.

"It's show time, Father." Jeffreys' lips curled. He turned to the three uniformed men and offered his wrists.

Father Francis winced as the shackles snapped. Then he listened to the boot heels clicking, accompanied by the pathetic shuffle-clank, shuffle-clank of the leg-irons all the way down the long hall.

"God help Ronald Jeffreys," Father Francis whispered.

At least Jeffreys had told the truth. He had not killed all three boys. And Father Francis knew this, not because Jeffreys had said so. He knew, because three days ago the faceless monster who had murdered Aaron Harper and Eric Paltrow had confessed to him through the black, wire-mesh confessional at St Margaret's. And because of his holy vows, he wasn't able to tell a single soul.

Not even Ronald Jeffreys.

Five miles outside Platte City, Nebraska
Friday, October 24

Nick Morrelli wished the woman beneath him wore less makeup. He listened to her soft moans—purrs really. Like a cat, she slithered against him, rubbing her silky thighs up and down the sides of his torso. She was more than ready for him. And yet, all he could think about was the blue powder smeared on her eyelids. Even with the lights out, it remained etched in his mind like fluorescent, glow-in-the-dark paint.

"Oh, baby, your body is so hard," she purred in his ear as she ran her long fingernails up his arms and over his back.

He slid off her before she discovered that not all of his body was hard. What was wrong with him? He licked her earlobe and nuzzled her neck, then moved down to where he really wanted to be. Instinctively, his mouth found one of her breasts. He ravished it with soft, wet kisses. He loved those sounds a woman made—the short little gasp, then the low moan. He waited for them, then wrapped his tongue around her nipple and sucked it into his mouth. Her back arched, and she quivered. Normally, that reaction alone would immediately give him an erection. Tonight, nothing.

Jesus, was he losing his touch? No, he was too young to be having this problem. After all, he was four years away from forty.

"Ooh, lover, don't stop!"

He didn't even realize he *had* stopped.

He began the descent down her body, devouring her with kisses and nibbles. Her body squirmed beneath his touch. She was writhing and gasping for breath even before his teeth tugged at her lace panties. He kissed his way to the inside of her thighs. Suddenly, a sound stopped him. He strained to hear from under the bedcovers.

"No, please don't stop," she groaned, pulling him back into her.

There it was again. Pounding. Someone was at the front door.

"I'll be right back." Nick stumbled out of bed. He pulled on jeans as he checked the clock on the nightstand—10:36 p.m.

When he opened the door, Nick recognized Hank Ashford's son, though he couldn't recall his name. The boy was sixteen or seventeen, a linebacker on the football team.

"Sheriff Morrelli, you have to come…on Old Church Road…please, you have to…"

"Is someone hurt?" The crisp night air stung Nick's bare skin. It felt good.

"No, it's not…he's not hurt… Oh, God, Sheriff, it's awful." The boy looked back toward his car. It was only then that Nick saw the girl in the front seat. He could see she was crying.

"What's going on?"

"In the tall grass…we found…we found a body."

"Hang on a minute."

"Nick, what is it?"

The voice from the top of the stairs startled him. He had forgotten about Angie.

"I've got to check something out."

"Is someone hurt?"

"I don't know."

"Did someone find the Alverez boy?" she asked.

The boy had been missing since Sunday, gone, taken before he began his newspaper route.

"No, I don't think so," Nick told her. Even the FBI was certain the boy had more than likely been taken by his father, who they were still trying to locate. It was a simple custody battle.

"I might be a while, but you're welcome to stay."

Old Church Road was filled with ruts from the rains of the week before. The gravel popped against the Jeep as Nick weaved from side to side, avoiding the deep gashes in the road.

"What exactly were you two doing out on this washboard?" As soon as he said it, he realized the obvious. He didn't need to be seventeen to remember all the benefits of an old deserted gravel road. "Never mind," he added before either of them had time to answer. "Just tell me where I'm going."

"It's about another mile, just past the bridge. There's a pasture road that runs along the river."

Nick slowed down as the Jeep bumped across the wood-slatted bridge. He found the pasture road even before Ashford pointed it out.

"All the way down to the trees?" Nick glanced at Ashford, who nodded and stared straight ahead. As they approached the shelterbelt, the girl, who sat between them, hid her face in the boy's sweatshirt.

Nick stopped, killed the engine, but left on the headlights. He reached across the two of them and pulled a flashlight from the glove compartment.

"That door sticks," he said to Ashford. He watched the two exchange a glance. Neither made any attempt to leave the Jeep.

"You never said we'd have to look at it again," the girl whispered to Ashford as she clung to his arm.

Nick stood outside the Jeep, waiting. The boy's eyes met his, but still he made no motion to leave the Jeep. Instead of insisting, Nick pointed the flashlight toward an area down by the riverbank. Ashford's eyes followed. He hesitated, looked back at Nick and nodded.

The tall grass swished around Nick's knees, camouflaging the mud that sucked at his boots. Jesus, it was dark out. Even the orange moon hid behind a gauze of clouds. Leaves rustled behind him. He spun around and shot a stream of light from tree to tree. Was there movement? There, in the brush? He could have sworn a shadow ducked from the light. Or was it just his imagination?

It was an effort to walk, pulling each foot out and carefully placing it to avoid slipping.

"Damn it," he muttered. "This better be good." He was going to be mad as hell if he found a group of teenagers playing hide-and-seek.

The flashlight caught something glittering in the mud, close to the water. He locked his eyes on the spot and quickened his pace. He was almost there, almost out of the tall grass. Suddenly, he tripped. He lost his balance and crashed down hard, with his elbows breaking his fall. The flashlight flew out of his hand and into the black water, a tunnel of light spiraling to the bottom.

The sucking mud pulled at him as he pushed himself to his hands and knees. A rancid smell clung to him, more than just the stench of the river. The silvery object lay almost within reach, and now he could tell it was a cross-shaped medallion. The chain was broken.

He glanced back to see what had caused his fall. Something solid. But not more than a yard away was a small, white body nestled in the mud and leaves.

Nick scrambled to his feet, his knees weak. The smell was more noticeable now, and it filled the air. He approached the body slowly. Then he saw the boy's slashed throat and mangled chest, the skin ripped open and peeled back. That was when his stomach lurched and his knees caved in.

"All it takes is one bad apple," Christine Hamilton pounded out on the keyboard, in the Platte City office of the *Omaha Journal*. Then she hit the delete key and watched the words disappear. She leaned back to steal a glance at the hall clock—the lighted beacon in the tunnel of darkness. Almost eleven o'clock. Thank God, Timmy had a sleepover.

Janitorial services had shut off the hall light again. Just another reminder of how important the "Living Today" section was. At the end of the dark hall, she saw the newsroom's light glowing under the door that segregated the departments. Just on the other side of that door, news was being made while she fussed over apple pie.

She whipped open a file folder and flipped through the notes and recipes. Over a hundred ways to slice, dice, puree and bake apples, and she couldn't care less. She knew her journalism degree was rusty, thanks to her husband's pigheadedness and his insistence that he wear the pants in the family. Too bad Bruce couldn't keep his pants on.

She shoved away from the computer terminal and raked her fingers through her thick mass of blonde hair.

She ignored the building's no smoking rule and slapped a cigarette out of the pack she kept in her handbag. Quickly, she lit it and sucked in, waiting for the nicotine to calm her. Before she exhaled, she heard a door slam. She smashed the cigarette into a dessert plate that bulged with too many lipstick-covered butts for a person trying to quit.

Footsteps echoed down the hall. Pete Dunlap, the duty night editor, entered the room.

"Hamilton. Good, you're still here." Pete had been with the *Omaha Journal* for almost fifty years. Despite the white hair, bifocals and arthritic hands, he was one of the few who could single-handedly put out the paper.

"Bailey called in sick. Russell's still finishing up on Congressman Neale's sex scandal, and I just sent Sanchez to cover a three-car smashup on Highway 50. There's some ruckus out by the river on Old Church Road in Sarpy County. I know you're not part of the news team, Hamilton, but would you mind checking it out?"

In the dark parking lot, Christine twirled once and shouted, "Yes!" to the concrete wall. This was her chance to get on the other side of the door, to go from recipes and household anecdotes to real news. Whatever was happening out at the river, she planned to capture all the nitty-gritty drama. And if there was no story…well, surely a good reporter could dig something up.

The rancid smell clung to Nick. He wanted to crawl out of his clothes, but the scent of river and blood was already soaked deep into his pores. He peeled off his shirt and thanked Bob Weston for the FBI windbreaker.

So little time had passed and yet the scene looked pre-Halloween. Blinding searchlights teetered from branches. Yellow tape flapped around trees. The sizzle and smoke of night flares mixed with that awful smell of death. There was a crowd of FBI agents and uniformed cops. And in the middle of the macabre scene lay the little white ghost of a boy, asleep in the grass.

In his two years as sheriff, Nick Morrelli had pulled three victims from car crashes. He had witnessed one gunshot wound. He had broken up numerous fistfights, sustaining his own cuts and bruises. Nothing, however, had prepared him for this.

"Channel Nine is here." Eddie Gillick, one of his deputies, pointed at the new set of headlights bumping down the path. The bright orange nine emblazoned on the top of the van glowed in the dark.

"Shit. How did they find out?"

"Police scanner. Probably have no idea what's going on, just that something is."

"Get Lloyd and Adam to keep them as far from that line of trees as possible. No cameras, no interviews, no sneak peeks. That goes for the rest of the bloodsuckers when they get here."

"Oh, good. Another fuckin' set of tire tracks," Weston said to the agents who were on their knees working in the mud, but he looked at Nick to make sure he knew the comment was meant for him.

Weston made it no secret he thought Nick was a small-town hick of a sheriff. They had been at each other's throats since Sunday when Danny Alverez had disappeared into thin air, leaving behind a brand-new bike and a bagful of undelivered newspapers. Nick had wanted to call in the masses to search fields and parks, while Weston had insisted they wait for a ransom note that never arrived. Nick had succumbed to Weston's twenty-five years of FBI experience instead of listening to his gut.

Nick saw George Tillie making his way through the crowd, and he was relieved to see the familiar face. George looked as if he had come straight out of bed. He took George's elbow and let the old coroner lean on him as they plodded through the mud and the crowd.

An officer with a Polaroid camera flashed one last picture of the scene, then made room for them. One look at the boy, and George froze.

"Oh, dear God. Not again."

As she skidded into the pasture road Christine Hamilton's excitement grew. Rescue vehicles, two TV vans, five sheriff cruisers and a slew of other unmarked vehicles were scattered at haphazard angles in the mud. Three sheriff's deputies guarded the scene, which was cordoned off with yellow crime-scene tape. Crime-scene tape—this was serious.

Then she remembered the kidnapping—the paperboy whose face had been plastered over every newscast and newspaper since the beginning of the week. Had a ransom drop been made? There were rescue units. Perhaps a rescue was in progress.

She jumped from the car. Immediately the mud swallowed her leather pumps, refusing to surrender them. She kicked out of her shoes, threw them into the back of the car and padded her way in stockinged feet to the crowd of news media. Tall grass and a mass of uniformed bodies blocked any view of what was going on.

Christine recognized Deputy Eddie Gillick in the line. She approached slowly, making certain he saw her.

"Deputy Gillick? Hi, it's Christine Hamilton. Remember me?"

"Mrs. Hamilton. Sure, I remember. You're Tony's daughter. What brings you out here?"

"I work for the *Omaha Journal* now."

She noticed Gillick's slicked-back hair, not a strand out of place, and the overpowering smell of aftershave lotion. Even the pencil-thin mustache was meticulously trimmed. His uniform looked wrinkle-free. A quick glance showed no wedding band. She'd take a chance that he considered himself a bit of a lady's man.

"I can't believe how muddy it is out here. Silly me. I even lost my shoes."

Gillick checked out the feet, and she was pleased when his eyes ran the length of her long legs. The uncomfortably short skirt would finally pay for its discomfort.

"You should be careful you don't catch cold." One more look, this time his eyes took in more than just her legs. She felt them stop at her breasts and found herself arching her back to split the blazer open just a little more to accommodate him.

She leaned in close to him, despite the smell of Brylcream. Even without shoes she was almost his height. "I know you're not allowed to discuss anything about the Alverez boy," she whispered, her lips close to his ear.

"How did you know?" He turned to see if anyone was listening.

Bingo. She'd hit the jackpot. Careful now. Cool and calm. Don't blow it.

"Oh, you know I can't say who my sources are, Eddie."

"Sure, of course."

"You probably didn't even get a chance to look at the scene. You know, being stuck out here doing the real dirty work."

"Oh, no. I got more than an eyeful." He puffed out his chest.

"The boy's in pretty bad shape, huh?"

"Yeah, looks like the son of a bitch gutted him," he whispered without a hint of emotion.

She felt the blood rush from her head. Her knees went weak. The boy was dead. Murdered. To quote Deputy Gillick, "gutted"! She had her first big story, yet in the pit of her stomach the butterflies had turned into cockroaches.

The Platte City Courthouse Building
Saturday, October 25

"Morrelli." Bob Weston came into Nick's office without knocking. The FBI man plopped down in the chair across from Nick. "You should go home. Shower, change clothes. You stink."

"What about the ex-husband?"

Weston shook his head. "I'm a father, Nick. I don't care how pissed off he might be with his wife—I just don't think a father could do that to his kid."

"So where do we begin?"

"I'd start with a list of known sex offenders, pedophiles and child pornographers."

"That could be a long list."

"Excuse me, Nick," Lucy Burton interrupted from the doorway. "Just wanted to let you know that all four Omaha TV stations and both Lincoln stations are downstairs with camera crews. There's also a hall full of newspaper and radio people. They're asking about a statement or press conference."

"Shit," Nick muttered. "Thanks, Lucy. We've avoided the press all week," Nick said, returning his gaze to Weston. "We're gonna have to talk to them."

"I agree. You need to talk to them."

"Me? Why me? I thought you were the hotshot expert."

"That was when it was a kidnapping. Now it's a homicide, Morrelli. Sorry, this is your ball game."

Nick slumped back in his chair.

"Look, Morrelli, I've been thinking. This being a kid and all, maybe I could request someone to help you put together a profile."

"What do you mean?"

"We have experts who can put together a psychological profile of this guy. Narrow things down for you. Give you a fuckin' idea of who this asshole is."

"Yeah, that would help. That would be good."

"I've been reading about this Special Agent O'Dell, an expert in profiling murderers practically right down to their shoe size. I could call Quantico."

"How soon do you think they could get someone here?"

"Don't let George Tillie cut up the boy yet. I'll call right now and see if we can get someone here Monday morning. Maybe even O'Dell."

Weston stood up. Nick untangled his legs and stood, too, surprised that his knees were strong enough to hold him.

Deputy Hal Langston met Weston at the door. "Thought you guys might be interested in this morning's edition of the *Omaha Journal*." Hal unfolded the paper and held it up. The headline screamed in tall, bold letters, BOY'S MURDER ECHOES JEFFREYS' STYLE.

Weston ripped the paper from him and began reading out loud.

> " 'Last night, a boy's body was found along the Platte River, off Old Church Road. Early reports suggest the still-unidentified boy was stabbed to death. A deputy at the scene, who will remain anonymous, said, 'It looked like the bastard gutted him.' Gaping chest wounds were a trademark of serial killer Ronald Jeffreys, who was executed in July of this year. Police have yet to make a statement concerning the boy's identity and the cause of death.'

"Goddamn it, Morrelli. You're gonna have to put a gag order on your men."

"It gets worse," Hal said, looking at Nick. "The byline is Christine Hamilton."

Weston looked from Hal to Nick. "Oh, please don't tell me she's one of the little harem you're bopping?"

"No," Nick said slowly. "Christine Hamilton is my sister."

Maggie O'Dell kicked off her muddy running shoes in the foyer before her husband, Greg, reminded her to do so. She missed their tiny, cluttered apartment in Richmond, despite surrendering to the much-needed convenience of living between Quantico and Washington.

She peeled off the damp sweatshirt and shot it into the laundry room as she passed on her way to the kitchen. She opened the refrigerator, grabbed a bottle of water and slammed the door, now shivering in only running shorts, a sweat-drenched T-shirt and sports bra that stuck to her like an extra layer of skin.

The phone rang. She searched the spotless counters and grabbed it off the unused microwave before the fourth ring.

"Hello."

"O'Dell, it's Kyle Cunningham."

She ran her fingers through her wet mass of short, dark hair and stood up straight, his voice setting her at attention.

"Hi. What's up?"

"I just received a phone call from the Omaha field office. They have a murder victim, a little boy. Some of the wounds are characteristic of a serial killer in the same area about six years ago."

"He's on the prowl again?"

"No, the serial killer was Ronald Jeffreys. I don't know if you remember the case. He murdered three boys."

"Yes, I remember," she interrupted him, knowing he hated long explanations. "Wasn't he executed in June or July of this year?"

"Yes…yes, in July, I believe."

"So this might be a copycat."

"It could be. The point is, they requested a profiler. Matter of fact, Bob Weston requested you specifically."

"So I'm a celebrity even in Nebraska? When do I leave?"

"Not so fast, O'Dell." She clutched the phone and waited for the lecture. "I'm sure Weston's pile of glowing reports about you didn't include the last case file."

"I certainly hope you're not going to hold the Stucky case over my head every time I go out into the field." The quiver in her voice sounded angry. That was good—anger was good, better than weakness.

"You know that's not what I'm doing, Maggie. I'm simply concerned. You never took a break after Stucky. You didn't even see the bureau psychologist."

"Kyle, I'm okay," she lied. "I've seen plenty of blood and guts in the past eight years. There's not much that shocks me anymore."

"That's exactly what I'm worried about. I don't care how tough you think you are—when the blood and guts get sprayed all over you, it's a little different than walking in on it."

She didn't need the reminder. Fact was, it didn't take much to conjure up the image of Albert Stucky hacking those women to death—his bloody death-play performed just for Maggie. His voice still came to her in the middle of the night: "I want you to watch. If you close your eyes, I'll just kill another one and another and another."

She had a degree in psychology. She didn't need a psychologist to tell her why she couldn't sleep at night, why the images still haunted her. She hadn't even been able to tell Greg about that night; how could she tell a complete stranger?

Of course, Greg hadn't been around when she had staggered back to her hotel room. He'd been miles away when she tore pieces of Lydia Barnett's brain out of her hair and scrubbed Melissa Stonekey's blood and skin out of her pores. When she had dressed her own wound, an unsightly slit across her abdomen. And it wasn't the kind of thing you talked about over the phone.

"How was your day, dear? Mine? Oh, nothing too exciting. I just watched two women get gutted and bludgeoned to death."

No, the real reason she hadn't told Greg was that he would have gone nuts. He had ranted and raved once before when she had confided in him. It had been the last time she had talked about her work. He didn't seem to mind the lack of communication. He didn't even notice her absence beside him in bed at night, when she paced the floor to avoid the images, to quiet the screams that still echoed in her head. The lack of intimacy with her husband allowed her to keep her scars—physical and mental—to herself.

"Maggie?"

"I need to keep working, Kyle. Please don't take that away from me."

There was silence.

"I'll fax over the details," he finally said. "Your flight leaves in the morning at six o'clock. Call me if you have any questions."

She listened to the click and waited for the dial tone. With the phone still pressed against her ear, she sighed, then breathed deeply. The front door slammed and she jumped.

"Maggie?"

"I'm in the kitchen."

"Hey, babe."

Greg came around the counter. He started to hug her, but stopped when he noticed the perspiration. He manufactured a smile to disguise his disgust. When had he started using his lawyer acting talents on her?

"We have reservations for six-thirty. Are you sure you have time to get ready?"

She glanced at the wall clock. It was only four. How bad did he think she looked?

"No problem," she said, guzzling more water and purposely letting it dribble down her chin.

The phone rang, and Greg reached for it.

"Let it ring," she said. "It's a fax from Director Cunningham." She raced to the den, checked the caller ID, then flipped on the fax.

"Why is he faxing you on a Saturday?"

"He's faxing some details on a case I've been asked to profile."

"Tonight was supposed to be a nice quiet dinner, just the two of us."

"And it will be. It may just need to be an early night. I have a six o'clock flight in the morning."

Silence. One, two, three…

"Damn it, Maggie. It's our anniversary. This was supposed to be our weekend together."

"No, that was last weekend, only you forgot and played in the golf tournament."

"Oh, I see. So this is payback."

"No, it's not payback. It's work."

"Work, right. That's convenient. Call it what you want. It's payback."

"A little boy has been murdered, and I might be able to help find the psycho who did it."

"Tell them to send someone else, Maggie. We need this weekend together."

She looked into his gray eyes and wondered when they had lost their color. She searched for a flicker of the intelligent, compassionate man she had married nine years ago when they were both college seniors ready to make their marks on the world. She would track down the criminals, and he would defend the helpless victims.

"Tell them to send someone else, or we're finished."

"If this one trip means we're finished, then maybe we've been finished for a long time!"

Sunday, October 26

And so it begins, he thought as he sipped the scalding-hot tea.

The front-page headline belonged on the *National Enquirer* and not a newspaper as respectable as the *Omaha Journal*. FROM THE GRAVE, SERIAL KILLER STILL GRIPS COMMUNITY WITH BOY'S RECENT MURDER. The byline was Christine Hamilton again. He recognized the name from the "Living Today" section. Why would they give the story to a newcomer, a rookie?

Quickly, he turned the pages, searching for the rest of the story, which continued on page ten, column one. The entire page was filled with connecting articles. There was a school photo of the boy. Beside it ran an in-depth saga of the boy's sudden disappearance during his early-morning paper route just a week ago. The article told how the FBI and the boy's mother had waited for a ransom note that never came. Then, finally, Sheriff Morrelli had found the body in a pasture along the river.

He glanced back at the paragraph. Morrelli? No, this was Nicholas Morrelli, not Antonio. How nice, he thought, for father and son to share the same experience.

The article went on to point out the similarities to the murders of three boys in the same small community over six years ago. And how the bodies, strangled and stabbed to death, had each been discovered days later in different wooded, isolated areas.

He used the fillet knife to scoop jelly and spread it on his burnt English muffin. The stupid toaster hadn't worked right for weeks, but it was better than going down to the kitchen and having breakfast with the others.

The room was very plain, white walls and hardwood floors. The small twin-size bed barely accommodated his six-foot frame. On the nightstand stood the most elaborate of his furnishings, an ornate lamp, the base a detailed relief of cherubs and nymphs tastefully arranged. It was one of the few things he had splurged on and purchased for himself with his meager paycheck. That and the three paintings. Of course, he could only afford framed reproductions. They hung on the wall opposite his bed so he could look at them while he drifted off to sleep.

He finished his breakfast and meticulously cleaned the table, no crumb escaping his quick swipes with the damp rag. From his small, brown-stained bathroom sink he removed the pair of Nikes, now scrubbed clean, not a hint of mud left. Still, he wished he had taken them off sooner. He patted them dry and set them aside to wash the one plate he called his own, a fragile, hand-painted Noritake.

His morning ritual complete, he got down on his hands and knees and pulled a wooden box from under the bed. He laid the box on the small table and ran his fingers over the lid's intricate carving. Carefully, he cut out the newspaper articles. He opened the box and put the folded articles inside on top of the other newspaper clippings, some of which were just beginning to yellow. He checked the other contents: a bright white linen cloth, two candles and a small container of oil. Then he licked the remnants of jelly off the fillet knife and returned it to the box, laying it gently on the soft cotton of a pair of boy's underpants.

Timmy Hamilton pushed his mom's fingers away from his face as the two of them hesitated on the steps of St Margaret's. It was bad enough that he was late. He didn't need his mom fussing over him in front of his friends.

"Come on, Mom. Everybody can see."

"Is this a new bruise?" Christine held his chin and gently tilted his head.

"I ran into Chad at soccer practice. It's no big deal." He put his hand on his hip as if to conceal the even bigger bruise hidden there.

"You need to be more careful, Timmy. You bruise so easily. I must have been out of my mind when I agreed to let you play." She opened her handbag and began digging.

"I'm gonna be late. Church starts in fifteen minutes."

"I thought I had your registration form and check for the campout."

"Mom, I'm late already."

"Okay, okay." She snapped the bag shut. "Just tell Father Keller I'll put it in the mail tomorrow."

"Can I go now?"

"Yes."

"You sure you don't want to check the tags on my underwear or something?"

"Smart-ass." She laughed and swatted him on the butt.

He liked it when she laughed, something she didn't do much of since his dad had left. When she laughed, the lines in her face softened, denting her cheeks with dimples. She became the most beautiful woman he knew.

Timmy knocked on the ornate door to the church vestibule. When no one answered, he opened it slowly and peeked in before entering. He found a cassock in his size among those hanging in the closet, and he ripped it from the hanger, trying to make up for lost time. He threw his jacket to a chair across the room, then jumped, startled by the priest kneeling quietly next to the chair. His rod-straight back faced Timmy, but the boy recognized Father Keller's dark hair curling over his collar. His thin frame towered over the chair, though he was on his knees. Despite Timmy's jacket almost hitting him, the priest remained still and quiet.

Finally, his elbow lifted to make the sign of the cross. He stood without effort and turned to Timmy, taking the jacket and draping it carefully over the chair's arm.

"Does your mom know you throw around your Sunday clothes?" He smiled with white, even teeth and bright blue eyes.

"Sorry, Father. I didn't see you when I came in. I was afraid I was late."

"No problem. We have plenty of time." He tousled Timmy's hair, his hand lingering on his head. It was something Timmy's dad used to do.

Father Keller seemed like a best friend instead of a priest. Sometimes on Saturdays, he played football with the boys down at the park, allowing himself to be tackled and getting just as muddy as the rest of them. At camp, he told gory ghost stories—the kind parents forbid. Sometimes after mass, Father Keller traded baseball cards. He had some of the best ones, really old ones like Jackie Robinson and Joe DiMaggio.

Timmy waited for Father Keller to put on the last of his garments. The priest checked his image in the floor-length mirror, then turned to Timmy.

"Ready?"

"Yes, Father," he said and followed the priest through the small hallway to the altar.

Timmy couldn't help smiling at the bright white Nikes peeking out from under the priest's long black cassock.

The information Maggie O'Dell had accessed from the Nebraska Tourism website described Platte City (population 3,500) as a growing bedroom community for many who worked in Omaha (twenty miles to the northeast) and Lincoln (thirty miles to the southwest). That explained the beautiful, well-manicured homes and neighborhoods—many recently built—despite the non-existence of any nearby industry.

Small shops lined the downtown square: a post office, Wanda's Diner, a movie theater, something called Paintin' Place, a small grocery store and, yes, even a drugstore/soda fountain. Bright red awnings hung over some of the shops. Others had window boxes with geraniums still in bloom. In the center of the square, the redbrick courthouse towered over the other buildings. Built during an era when pride overrode expense, its façade included a detailed relief of Nebraska's past—covered wagons and plow horses separated by the scales of justice.

Inside the lobby of the courthouse, Maggie's heels clicked on the marble floor, sending an echo all the way to the vaulted cathedral ceiling. She scanned the wall directory. The County Sheriff's department resided on the third floor.

The department appeared empty, though the smell of freshly brewed coffee and the hum of a copy machine seeped in from one of the back rooms. The wall clock showed eleven-thirty. Maggie checked her watch. She was still on eastern time. She reset it as she walked to the windows facing south. The thick gray clouds now blocked any hint of sun or blue sky. Below, the streets remained quiet. It wasn't noon, and she was already exhausted. She was drained from her battle with Greg and another sleepless night avoiding visions of Albert Stucky. Then, this morning, the turbulent flight had jerked and jolted her thousands of feet above control. She hated flying, and it never got any easier.

She wished she had checked into a hotel first and eaten some lunch instead of coming directly here. But she was ready to dig in, having spent the hours in the air preoccupying herself with details of Ronald Jeffreys. The recent murder resembled Jeffreys' style, right down to the jagged X carved into the boy's chest. Copycats were often meticulous, duplicating every last detail to amplify the thrill.

"Can I help you?"

Maggie spun around. The young woman who appeared out of nowhere was far from what Maggie had expected of someone working in a sheriff's office. Her long hair was too tall and stiff, her knit skirt too short and tight. She looked more like a teenager ready for a date.

"I'm here to see Sheriff Nicholas Morrelli."

The woman eyed Maggie suspiciously, keeping her post in the doorway as though guarding the back offices. "What exactly is it that you need to talk to Nick…to Sheriff Morrelli about?"

Maggie had reached into her jacket pocket, ready to flip out her badge, when two men came noisily in the front door. The older man wore a brown deputy's uniform, the pants impeccably pressed, the tie cinched tight at his neck. The younger was wearing a gray T-shirt drenched in sweat, shorts and running shoes. His dark brown hair, though short, was tousled, strands wet against his forehead. Despite his disheveled look, he was handsome and definitely in good shape, with long muscular legs, slender waist and broad shoulders.

Both men stopped talking as soon as they saw Maggie. They looked from Maggie to the young woman still at her post in the doorway.

"Hi, Lucy. Is everything okay?" the younger man said as his eyes scanned the length of Maggie's body. When his eyes finally met hers, he smiled as if she had met his approval.

"I was just trying to find out what this lady—"

"I'm here to see Sheriff Morrelli," Maggie interrupted. She brought out her badge and flipped it open. "I'm with the FBI."

"You're Special Agent O'Dell?" the younger man said.

"Yes, that's right."

He wiped his hand on his T-shirt and extended it to her. "I'm Nick Morrelli. This is Deputy Eddie Gillick, and I guess you already met Lucy Burton. I am really sorry I wasn't here when you arrived. Actually, I just got back from Omaha. I ran in the Corporate Cup Run." He seemed eager to explain, almost uncomfortable, as though he had been caught at something he shouldn't be doing. He shifted from one foot to another.

"It's a fund-raiser for the American Lung Association…or maybe it's the American Heart Association. I can't remember. Anyway, it's for a good cause."

"You don't owe me an explanation, Sheriff Morelli," she said, although she was pleased that her presence seemed to demand one.

"After over thirty-six straight hours on the case," Morrelli continued, "we decided to take a break today. I really didn't think you'd be here until tomorrow. You know, it being Sunday."

"My superiors gave me the impression that time may be important in this case. You are still holding the body for my examination, aren't you?"

"Yes, of course. We're using the hospital morgue. If you'd like, I can take you there."

"Thanks. But first, there's someplace else I'd like you to take me."

"Sure. You probably want to unpack. Are you staying here in town?"

"Actually, that's not what I meant. I'd like to see the scene of the crime." She watched Morrelli's face grow pale. "I'd like you to show me where you found the body."

Nick glanced at Agent O'Dell as he tried to keep the Jeep from sliding into the worst parts of the mud. Though she acted older, he guessed she was only in her late twenties, maybe early thirties—much too young to be an expert. Her age wasn't the only thing that disarmed him. Despite her cool, abrupt manner she was very attractive. And even the conservative-style suit couldn't hide what he suspected was a knockout body. Under ordinary circumstances he'd be preparing a full-throttled charm assault. But, Jesus, there was something about her that sent him into a tailspin. She carried herself with such poise, such confidence and self-assurance. She acted as though she knew what she was doing, which only made him more aware of his own lack of expertise. It was annoying as hell.

The Jeep jerked to a stop in front of the shelterbelt of trees. He heard O'Dell struggle with the door handle, the familiar click of metal against metal.

"Wait, that door sticks. I'll get it from the outside."

"Good idea."

He sloshed around to the other side of the Jeep. Back at the office he had taken a quick shower, put on jeans and traded the running shoes for the same boots he had worn during the night. Dry mud still clung to the expensive leather.

The Jeep's door opened easily from the outside.

"Hold on." He stopped her again. "I think I have some boots

back here." He stretched over the seat. The rubber work boots were within arm's reach.

"Are you sure those are necessary?"

"You'll never get anywhere in this mud. It's worse by the riverbank."

The area was still cordoned off by yellow tape strung from trees. Sections were torn, flapping in the breeze, a breeze that grew stronger as the fast-moving clouds rolled overhead.

Nick watched her step carefully around the impression of the small body that still remained pressed into the grass. She crouched down, examined the blades of grass, scooped up a fingerful of mud and sniffed it. Nick winced, remembering the rancid smell.

O'Dell stood and looked out at the river. The bank was only three or four feet away. The unusually high waters churned, slapping at the banks.

"Where did you find the medallion?" she asked.

"Here," he said, pointing to the plastic marker sunk into the mud, barely visible.

She looked at the spot, then back at the boy's resting place. It was only a couple of feet away.

"It was the boy's. His mother identified it," Nick explained. "The chain was broken. It must have gotten pulled off in the struggle."

"Except there was no struggle."

"Excuse me?"

"There wasn't a struggle."

"What makes you say that?"

"You fell here when you tripped, right?" she said, pointing to the torn grass and the indent in the mud.

"That's right," he admitted.

"The trampling around the perimeter is obviously from your deputies."

"And the FBI," Nick added defensively, though he knew she wasn't concerned with those details. "They were in charge until we ruled out a kidnapping."

"Other than this spot and where the body lay, there is no torn grass or any beaten down. The victim's hands and feet were bound when you found him?"

"Yeah, back behind him."

"My guess is that he was like that when they arrived here."

"So how did the chain get broken?"

"I don't know for sure. Maybe the killer pulled it off. It was a silver cross, right?"

She looked to him for assurance. He nodded, impressed that she had equipped herself with so many details from his report. She continued as if thinking out loud.

"Maybe the killer didn't like staring at it. Maybe he wasn't able to do what he wanted to do as long as the victim was wearing it. Its religious significance is some sort of protection. Perhaps the killer is religious enough to have known that and have been uncomfortable."

"A religious killer? Great."

"What other trace do you have?"

"Trace?"

"Other evidence—other objects, torn pieces of fabric or rope?"

"We did find a footprint."

"A footprint? Excuse me, Sheriff, I don't mean to sound skeptical, but how were you able to isolate a footprint? From what I can tell, there must have been over a dozen pairs of feet out here. How do you know that the prints you found weren't made by one of your men or the FBI?"

"Because none of us were barefoot." He moved closer to the river. He grabbed onto a tree branch just as his boots slid partway down the bank. When he looked up, O'Dell was standing over him.

"Right here." He pointed to the set of toes imprinted in the mud and highlighted with remnants of casting powder.

"There's no guarantee those are the killer's."

"Who else would be nuts enough to be out here without shoes?"

She grabbed the same branch and slid down next to him.

"You mind giving me a hand?" She extended a hand to him and he took it, allowing her to hang on while she bent down and stretched over the impression without sliding into the water.

Her hand was soft and small in his, but her grip was strong. Her jacket swung open, and he made himself look away. Jesus, she certainly didn't look like an FBI agent.

After a few seconds she pulled herself up and immediately released his hand. Back on solid ground, she started writing in her notebook.

"The puncture marks and the carving in the boy's chest were exactly like the Jeffreys murders," he said. "Do you think this is a copycat killer?"

"Yes."

"Why would anyone copycat a murder like this? For kicks?"

"I'm afraid I can't tell you that," O'Dell replied, looking up from the notebook and meeting his eyes. "What I can tell you is this guy is going to do it again. And probably soon."

The hospital's morgue was in the basement where every sound echoed off the white brick walls. Water pipes thumped and a fan wheezed in motion. Behind them, the elevator door squeezed shut. There was a whirl and a scrape as cables strained and pulled the car back up.

Maggie O'Dell stood back while Morrelli fumbled with a tangle of keys, then discovered the door to the morgue unlocked. He held it open for her, pressing his body against its weight and requiring her to squeeze past him. She wasn't sure whether it was intentional or not, but this was the second or third time he had arranged for their bodies to be within touching distance.

Usually her cool, authoritarian manner quickly put a stop to any unwanted advances. But Morrelli didn't seem to notice. Somehow, she imagined he treated every woman he met as a potential one-night stand. She knew his type and also knew that his flirting and flattery, along with the boyish charm and athletic good looks, probably got him as far as he wanted to go. It was annoying, but in Morrelli's case it seemed harmless.

Morrelli found the light switch, and, like dominoes falling, the rows of fluorescent lights blinked on, one after another. Immediately, the smell of ammonia hit her nostrils and burned her lungs. Everything was immaculately scrubbed. A stainless-steel table occupied the middle of the tiled floor. On one wall was a large double sink and a counter that held various tools. The opposite wall contained five refrigerated vaults.

She took off her jacket, laid it carefully over a stool and rolled up the sleeves.

She had brought with her a small black bag that contained everything she would need. She opened it and began laying its contents on the counter, first taking out the small jar of Vicks VapoRub and dabbing a bit around her nostrils. She had learned long ago that even refrigerated dead bodies gave off a smell that was worth avoiding. She started to close the lid, then stopped and turned to Morrelli, who watched from the door. She tossed him the jar.

"If you're going to stay, you might want to use some of this." He stared at the jar, then opened it, and followed her example.

"You really don't have to stay," she told him. He was beginning to look pale, and they hadn't even rolled out the body.

"No, I'll stay. I'll just…I don't want to be in your way."

She pulled out a recorder, checked the tape inside and set it for voice activation. She took out a Polaroid camera and made sure it was loaded with film.

"Which drawer?" she asked, turning to the vaults, ready to begin, her hands on her hips. She glanced back at Morrelli, who stared at the wall of drawers as if he hadn't realized they would actually have to take the body out.

He moved slowly, hesitantly, then unlatched the middle drawer and pulled. The metal rollers squealed then clicked as the drawer filled the room.

Maggie kicked the brake off the wheels of the steel table and rolled it under the drawer. It fit perfectly. Together they unhitched the drawer tray with the small body bag, so that it lay flat on the table. Then they pushed the table back to the middle of the room under the suspended lighting unit. As soon as she began unzipping the bag Morrelli retreated to the corner.

He had been a good-looking kid, Maggie found herself thinking. His reddish-blond hair was closely cropped. The freckles around his nose and cheeks stood out against the white, pasty skin. He was bruised badly under the neck, the strands of rope leaving indents just above the gaping slash.

She began by taking photos, close-ups of the puncture marks and the jagged X on the chest, then the blue and purple marks on the wrists and the slashed neck. With the recorder close by, she began documenting what she saw.

"The victim has bruise marks under and around his neck made by what looks to be a rope. It may have been tied. There appears to be an abrasion just under the left ear, perhaps from the knot."

She gently lifted the boy's head to look at the back of his neck. "Yes, the marks are all the way around the neck. This would indicate that the victim was strangled, then his throat slashed. The throat wound is deep and long, extending just below the ear to the other ear. Bruises on the wrists and ankles are similar to the neck. The same rope may have been used."

His hands were so small in hers. Maggie held them carefully, reverently, as she examined the palms. "There are deep fingernail marks on the inside of his palms. This would indicate that the victim was alive while some of the wounds were inflicted. The fingernails themselves appear to be clean…very clean."

"The victim has eight—no, nine—puncture marks in the chest cavity. They appear to have been made by a single-edged knife. Three are shallow. At least six are very deep, possibly hitting bone. One may have gone through the heart. Yet, there is very little…actually, there is no blood. Sheriff Morrelli, did it rain while the body was in the open?"

She looked up at him when he didn't answer. He was leaning against the wall, hypnotized by the small body on the table. "Sheriff Morrelli?"

This time he realized she was talking to him. He pushed off the wall and stood straight, almost at attention. "I'm sorry, what did you say?" His voice was hushed. He whispered as if not to wake the boy.

"Do you remember if it rained while the body was out in the open?"

"No, not at all. We had plenty of rain the week before."

"Did the coroner clean the body?"

"We asked George to hold off doing anything until you got here. Why?"

"Some of these wounds are deep. Even if they were made after the victim was dead, there would still be blood. If I remember correctly, there was plenty of blood at the crime scene in the grass and dirt."

"Lots of it. It took for ever to get it off my clothes."

"It's almost as if his body has been cleaned," she said. When she looked up, Morrelli was standing beside her.

"Are you saying the killer washed the body after he was finished?"

"Look at the carving in the chest." She gently poked her finger under the edge of the skin. "He used a different knife for this—one with a serrated edge. It ripped and tore the skin in some places. See here?" She ran her fingertip over the jagged skin.

"And these puncture wounds are deep." She stuck her finger into one to show him. "When you make a hole this size, this deep, it's going to bleed profusely until you plug it up. This one, I'm almost certain, went into the heart. We're talking major artery, major gusher. And the throat...Sheriff Morrelli?"

Morrelli was leaning against the table, his weight jerking the stainless steel and sending out a high-pitched screech of metal against tile. Maggie looked up at him. His face was white. Before she realized it, he slumped against her. She caught him by the waist, but he was too heavy, and she slipped to the floor with him, her knees crumpling under her.

"Morrelli, hey, are you okay?"

She squeezed out from under him and propped him against a table leg. He was conscious, but his eyes were glazed over. She climbed to her feet. She remembered seeing a pop machine next to the elevators. Fumbling for the correct change, she was there and back before Morrelli moved.

His legs were twisted underneath him. His head rested against the table. Now, at least, his eyes were more focused when she knelt next to him with the Pepsi can.

"Here."

"Thanks, but I'm not thirsty."

"No, for your neck. Here..." She reached down and laid the cold Pepsi can against the back of his neck.

"I can't believe I did that," he said. "I'm embarrassed."

"Don't be. I spent a lot of time on the floor before I got used to this stuff."

"How *do* you get used to it?" He looked back into her eyes, as if searching for the answer.

"I'm not sure. You just sort of disconnect, try not to think about it."

Before she could offer him a hand, Morrelli slowly got to his feet. He smiled at her and rubbed the cold condensation of the can against his forehead, leaving a wet streak.

"Do you mind meeting me up in the cafeteria when you're finished?"

"No, of course not. I won't be much longer."

He lifted the can to her as if in a toast, then walked out.

Maggie returned to the job in hand. She ran her eye over the body. When her gaze reached the head she leant forward. She could see something smeared on his brow.

She wiped a finger across the area and rubbed her fingers together under her nose. If the body had been washed clean, that meant the oily liquid had been applied after. Instinctively, Maggie checked the boy's blue lips and found a smear of the oil. Before she even looked, she knew she'd find more of the oil on the boy's chest, just above his heart. Perhaps all those years of catechism had finally paid off. Otherwise, she may have never recognized that someone, perhaps the killer, had given this boy the last rites.

Christine Hamilton tried to edit the article she had scribbled in her notebook while pretending to know the score of the soccer game being played on the field down below her.

A sudden burst of applause, hoots and whistles made her look up just in time to see the team of red-clad ten-year-old boys high-fiving each other. She had missed another goal, but when the small, red-haired boy looked up from the huddle, she gave him a smile and thumbs-up as if she had seen the whole thing.

She flipped a page and was about to return to her editing when she noticed three of the other divorced soccer moms whispering to each other. Instead of watching the game, they were pointing to the sidelines. Christine turned to follow their gaze and immediately saw what had distracted them. The man typified the cliché "tall, dark and handsome". When he finally looked over, she waved to him, enjoying the look of envy on the women's faces when he smiled at her and made his way up the bleachers to join her.

"What's the score?" Nick asked.

"I think it's five to three. You realize, don't you, that you just made me the envy of every drooling, divorced soccer mom here?"

"See, the things I do for you, and you repay me with such abuse."

"Abuse? I never hit you a day of your life," she told her younger brother. "Well, not hard."

"That's not what I meant, and you know it." He wasn't joking.

She sat up straight, preparing to defend herself despite the guilt gnawing at her stomach. Yes, she should have called him before she turned in the story. But what if he had asked her not to run it? That story had put her on the other side of the door. Rather than being stuck writing helpful household hints, she had two front-page articles in two days with her byline. And tomorrow she'd be sitting at her own desk in the city room.

"How about I make it up to you? Dinner tomorrow night? I'll fix spaghetti and meatballs with Mom's secret sauce."

He looked over at her, glanced at the notebook. "You just don't get it, do you?"

"Oh, come on, Nicky. You know how long I've been waiting to get out of the 'Living Today' section? If I hadn't filed that story, someone else would have."

"Really? And would they have quoted an officer who told them something off the record?"

"He never once said it was off the record. If Gillick told you otherwise, he's lying."

"Actually, I didn't know it was Eddie. Gee, Christine, you just gave away an anonymous source."

"Damn you, Nicky. You know how hard I'm trying. I'm a little rusty, but I can be a damn good reporter."

"Really? So far I think your reporting has been irresponsible."

"Oh, for crying out loud, Nicky. Just because you didn't like what I wrote doesn't make it irresponsible journalism."

"What about the headlines? Where do you get off comparing this murder to Jeffreys'?"

"Grow up, Nicky. Anyone with half a brain is going to compare this murder to Jeffreys'. I just wrote what everyone else is thinking. Are you saying I'm off target?"

"I'm saying we don't need another panic in a community that just started to feel like maybe their kids were safe again. And you made me look like a goddamn idiot, Christine."

"That's what this is really about. You don't care about a panic in the community. You're just worried about how you look. Why am I not surprised?"

It occurred to her that she must be getting old, because suddenly she regretted hurting his feelings. At the same time, she grew impatient with the way her brother approached things. He constantly took the easy way out, but then, why not? Everything seemed to be handed to Nick, from job opportunities to women. And he floated from one to the next without much effort, remorse or thought.

When their father retired as county sheriff and insisted that Nick run for office, Nick had left his professorship at the university without any hesitation. Without a hitch—and quite predictably, in fact—he had been elected to the post of county sheriff. Though Nick would be the first to admit it was only because of their father's name and reputation. But he didn't seem to mind. He just took things as they came.

Christine, on the other hand, had to scrape and claw for everything she wanted, especially since Bruce's departure. Well, this time she deserved the break she was getting.

"If it is a copycat murder, don't you think people deserve a warning?"

Nick didn't respond. Instead, he said, ""I just spent the afternoon at the morgue."

"Why?"

"Bob Weston called in an expert to help us come up with a profile—Special Agent Maggie O'Dell from Quantico. She got in this morning and was raring to get to work."

He glanced over at Christine, then did a double take when he noticed her scratching down something in her notebook.

"Jesus, Christine!" he spat out so suddenly it made her jump. "Isn't anything off the record with you?"

"If you wanted it off the record, you should have said so. Besides, by tomorrow everyone will know about Agent O'Dell when she starts asking questions. What are you worried about, Nicky? Calling in an expert is a good thing."

"Is it? Or will it just make me look like I don't know what the hell I'm doing?" He shot her another look. "Don't you dare print that."

"Relax. I'm not the enemy, Nicky. You know, Dad wasn't afraid to work with the news media."

"Yeah, well, I'm not Dad."

Now she had made him angry. She knew to stay away from the comparison, but if he didn't like it perhaps he shouldn't have followed in their father's footsteps. As usual, she simply sidestepped the subject.

"I'm just saying that Dad knew how to use the media to help."

"To help? Dad used the news media because he loved being in the limelight. There were so many leaks, it's amazing they ever caught Jeffreys."

"What leaks? What are you talking about?"

"Never mind," he said, glancing at her notebook.

"But they did catch Jeffreys, and Dad solved the case," she reminded him.

"Haven't you ever wondered...?" He hesitated. "Didn't you ever think it happened all too quickly...too neat and convenient?"

"What are you talking about?"

"Forget it," he said, standing up and stretching, closing the subject.

The man drove around the park again, this time slowly. The game was finally over. He pulled into a parking space, alone in the corner of the lot. He turned off the headlights and sat watching, listening to the music on the radio and waiting for the jerky strings of Vivaldi to smooth out and silence the throbbing in his temples.

It was happening again and so soon. He couldn't stop it, couldn't control it. And, worse, he didn't want to.

He watched the group of boys in grass-stained uniforms. They looked so happy, fresh from their victory, arms crossing around one another, hands patting each other on the back. They touched so carelessly, so casually. The memory came flooding back. He was eleven years old and his stepfather had made him join the Little League team, to get him out of the house on Saturday mornings. He knew it was only because his stepfather wanted to fuck his mother all morning.

He had accidentally walked in on them the Saturday before. He stood in the doorway of his mother's bedroom, paralyzed by the sight of his mother's skin, white and naked with the silver cross swinging between her big breasts. Her breasts wagged back and forth. She held herself up on her hands and knees while his stepfather rode her like a dog in heat.

It was his stepfather who saw him first. He yelled at him, panting and jerking, while his mother's eyes grew wide in horror. She twisted out from under his stepfather, falling and tumbling off the bed, grabbing for the sheet. It was then that he turned to run. He stumbled down the hall to his room. Just as he began to slam the door, his stepfather crashed through it.

It was the first time he had seen a grown man's penis, and it was horrible: huge, stiff and erect, protruding through the thick black hair. His stepfather grabbed him by the neck and shoved his face to the wall.

"You interested in watching? Or maybe you want some of this?"

His stepfather's fingers strangled his neck with one hand while he ripped his pajama pants with the other. Then he felt it. The intense pressure, the pain so stifling he thought his insides would explode. He wanted to scream. His cheek scraped against the rough texture of the bedroom wall. All he could do was stare at the crucifix hanging next to his face, while he waited for his stepfather to stop slamming into his small body…

A car horn blasted. He jumped and clutched the steering wheel. His palms were sweaty, his fingers trembling. He watched the boys getting into the cars and vans with their parents. How many of them were hiding secrets like his own? How many of them hid their bruises and scars? How many waited for some sort of relief, some sort of salvation from their misery? From their torture?

Then he saw the small boy waving to the others as he started up the sidewalk. He watched to see if he would walk home alone as he usually did.

It was starting to get dark. Several streetlights blinked on. He listened to the gravel grind beneath the cars as they pulled out and drove off. Headlights flicked on and blinded him as they turned to leave.

Half a block away, the boy still walked alone, tossing the soccer ball from one hand to the other. He looked thin and small in his baggy uniform, so very vulnerable.

The last car left the parking lot. He silenced Vivaldi. From his pocket he took a brilliant white handkerchief. Without him looking, his fingers found the small, glass vial from inside the glove compartment. Expertly, he cracked the vial and let it dampen the handkerchief. He grabbed the black ski mask and got out of the car, gently closing the door. His hands were no longer trembling. Yes, he was finally feeling back in control.

Monday, October 27

Maggie poured the rest of the Scotch from the small bottle to the plastic cup. The ice cubes cracked and tinkled against each other. She took a sip, closed her eyes and welcomed the lovely sting sliding down her throat.

It was after two in the morning, and she couldn't sleep. The small tabletop was covered with the Polaroid photos she had taken earlier. She attempted to put them in chronological order—hands tied, neck strangled then slashed, puncture wounds. This madman was methodical. He took his time. He cut, sliced and peeled back skin with frightening precision. Even the jagged X followed a specific diagonal from shoulder blade to belly button.

She scattered two file folders full of police reports and newspaper clippings. There were enough gory details to provide nightmares for a lifetime. Except it was impossible to have nightmares if you couldn't sleep.

She pulled her bare legs up, tucking her feet underneath her in an attempt to make herself comfortable in the hard chair. Her Green Bay Packers jersey barely covered her thighs, yet it was still the softest nightshirt she owned. It had become a sort of security blanket that made her feel at home no matter how many miles away.

She sifted through the scattered papers and examined her notes, several pages of details, small observations, some that would probably seem insignificant to anyone else. Eventually, she would pull them all together and create a profile of the killer. She had done it many times before.

She picked up the silver medallion and chain from the corner of the desk. It resembled the one Danny Alverez had worn. Though this one had been given to Maggie by her father for her first Holy Communion.

"As long as you wear this, God will protect you from any harm," her father had told her.

Until a month ago she had worn the medallion faithfully, perhaps out of routine and remembrance of her father rather than out of any sense of spirituality. But the night she watched Albert Stucky slaughter two women, Maggie had gone home and removed the medallion from around her neck. And although she couldn't bring herself to wear it anymore, she still carried it with her.

She heard a soft tap on the door. She got to her feet and padded quietly across the room. Through the peephole she could see Sheriff Morrelli. She opened the door, but just enough to look out at him.

"What's going on, Sheriff?"

"Sorry. I tried to call, but the night-desk clerk has been on the phone for over an hour."

"Is something wrong?"

"Another boy's missing."

"That's impossible," she said, but she knew that it wasn't. Albert Stucky had taken his fourth victim less than an hour after his third victim was discovered. The beautiful, blonde co-ed had been sliced in pieces, some of which were stuffed in take-out boxes and discarded in the Dumpster behind a restaurant Stucky had eaten at earlier that evening.

"I've got men going door-to-door in the neighborhood and searching alleys, parks, fields." He rubbed his hand over his exhausted face and scratched his bristled jaw. "The kid was walking home from a soccer game. He only had five blocks to walk."

"Maybe you should come in."

Maggie held the door open for him. He hesitated, then walked in slowly, staying in the entrance as he glanced around the room.

He turned back to Maggie, and his eyes dropped to her legs. She had forgotten about the short nightshirt.

"Sorry. Did I wake you?"

"No, I was still up."

She opened one of the dresser drawers and started digging for a pair of jeans. Finally, she found a pair and pulled them on.

"I was at that game," he said.

"What game?"

"The soccer game. The one the boy was walking home from. My nephew played. Jesus, Timmy probably knows this kid."

"Are you sure the boy didn't go home with a friend?"

"We called the other parents. His friends remember seeing him start walking up the sidewalk toward home. And we found his soccer ball. It's autographed by some famous soccer player. His mom says it's one of his most prized possessions. She insists he wouldn't have just left it."

He scraped a sleeve across his face. Maggie recognized the panic in his eyes. He wasn't prepared to handle a situation like this.

"Sheriff, maybe you should sit down."

"No, I'm fine."

"I insist." She reached up and grabbed him by the shoulders, gently shoving him into a chair. He looked as though he'd stand up again, thought better of it, then stretched out his long legs.

"We don't know for sure that this boy was taken. He could still show up at a friend's house. Or he may have run away."

"Okay." He sighed. "But you don't really believe he ran away, do you?"

"No. Probably not," she said. "I knew the killer would strike again. I just didn't think it would be *this* soon."

"So tell me where to begin. Have you had time to figure out anything about this guy?"

She stared at the montage of photos, notes and reports on the table.

"He's meticulous, in control. He takes his time, not only with the murder, but in cleaning up after himself. Though the cleaning isn't to hide evidence—it's part of his ritual. I think he may have done this before." She fingered through her notes. "He's definitely not young and immature," she continued. "There was no sign of struggle at the site, so the victim was tied beforehand. That means he has to be strong enough to carry a seventy-to-eighty-pound boy at least three hundred to five hundred yards. I'm guessing he's in his thirties, about six feet tall, two hundred pounds. He's white. He's educated and he's intelligent."

At some point during her description, Morrelli sat up, suddenly alert and interested in the mess she poked through.

"Remember at the hospital after I examined the Alverez boy, I told you he may have given the boy the last rites? That would mean the killer's Catholic, maybe not practicing, but his Catholic guilt is still strong. Strong enough that he's bothered by a medallion in the shape of a cross, so he rips it off. He performs extreme unction, perhaps to atone for his sin."

"He sounds like a real sicko. Is it possible he may have a record? Maybe child abuse or sexual molestation? Maybe even beating up a gay lover?"

"You assuming he's gay or that he's a pedophile?"

"An adult male who does this to little boys—isn't that a safe assumption?"

"I don't think he's gay, nor do I believe he's a pedophile."

"And you can tell all that just from the evidence we've found?"

"No. I'm guessing that from the evidence we haven't found. The victim didn't appear to be sexually abused. There were no traces of semen in the mouth or rectum, though he may have washed it off. There were no signs of any penetration, no indication of sexual stimulation. Even with Jeffreys' victims, only one—Bobby Wilson," she said, checking her notes. "Only the Wilson boy showed signs of sexual abuse and those seemed very obvious. Multiple penetration, lots of tearing and bruising."

"Wait a minute. If this guy is only copying Jeffreys, how can we be sure any of what he does is an indication of who he is?"

"Copycats choose murders that often play out their own fantasies. Sometimes they add their individual touches. I can't find any indications that Jeffreys gave his victims the last rites, though it could easily have been overlooked."

"I do know he asked for a priest to hear his confession before he was executed," said Nick.

"How do you know that?"

"My dad was the sheriff who brought in Jeffreys. Well, he had a front-row seat at the execution."

"Is it possible to ask him some questions?"

"He and my mom bought an RV a few years ago. They travel year-round. They check in from time to time, but I don't know how to get hold of them. I'm sure once they hear about this, he'll be in touch, but it may take a while."

"I wonder if it's possible to track down the priest?"

"No problem. Father Francis is still here at St Margaret's. Though I don't know what help he could be. It's not likely he'll share Jeffreys' confession."

"I'd still like to talk to him."

The phone started ringing. Timmy Hamilton scrambled to his feet to answer it.

"Hello?"

"Timmy? This is Mrs. Calloway—Chad's mom. Is your mom there?"

He almost blurted out that Chad had hit him first. If Chad said it was the other way around, he was lying. Instead, he said, "Just a minute. I'll get her."

Chad Calloway was a bully, but if Timmy had told his mom that Chad had purposely inflicted the bruises, she would have most definitely made him quit soccer. And now the bully had probably lied about his own bruises.

Timmy knocked on the bathroom door.

"Was that the phone?" Christine came out smelling good and bringing a trail of perfume with her.

"It's Mrs. Calloway."

"Who?"

"Mrs. Calloway, Chad's mom."

She squinted at him, her eyebrows raised as she waited for more.

"I don't know what she wants." He shrugged and followed her to the phone.

"This is Christine Hamilton. Yes, of course." She spun around to Timmy and mouthed, "Calloway?"

"She's Chad's mom," he whispered. She never listened to him.

"Yes, you're Chad's mom."

He couldn't tell what Mrs. Calloway was telling his mom. She paced as she normally did while on the phone. Then suddenly, she stopped and gripped the phone. Here it was. He needed to prepare his story. Wait a minute. He didn't need a story. The truth was, Chad had picked on him. And for no real reason, other than he liked it.

"Thank you for calling, Mrs. Calloway."

His mom hung up the phone and stared out the window. He couldn't tell whether she was angry.

"Timmy, one of your teammates is missing."

"What?"

"Matthew Tanner never came home last night after the soccer game."

So it had nothing to do with Chad!

"Some of the other soccer parents are meeting at the Tanner house this morning to help out. Go use the bathroom, and I'll take you to school. I don't want you walking today."

"Okay." Poor Matthew, he found himself thinking. Too bad Chad couldn't have been the one taken.

Christine couldn't believe her luck. She called Taylor Corby, the news editor, her new boss. When she told him about Matthew Tanner, Corby listened.

"Christine, you know what that means? If you have copy for this evening's paper, we will have scooped the other media three days in a row."

"I still need to convince Mrs. Tanner to let me interview her."

"Interview or not, you already have enough for a great story. Just make sure you substantiate your facts."

"Of course."

Brightly colored stained-glass figures stared down from their heavenly perch. The scent of burning incense and candle wax filled Maggie's nostrils.

"Everything okay?" Nick asked.

He had left her hotel room at five o'clock in the morning to go home, shower, shave and change clothes. When he arrived two hours later to pick her up, she hardly recognized him. His short hair was neatly combed back. His face was clean-shaven, and the white scar on his chin—even more pronounced—added a rugged edge to his good looks. Underneath his denim jacket he wore a white shirt and black tie with crisp blue jeans and shiny black cowboy boots.

She looked around the church. It seemed large for a town of Platte City's size, with rows and rows of wooden pews. She couldn't imagine all of them being filled.

"It seems so big," she said, trying to explain her distraction.

"It's relatively new. The old church was a small country parish about five miles south of town," he told her. "Platte City's grown, practically doubled in the last ten years."

"You folks need some help?" A man appeared from a curtain behind the altar.

"We're looking for Father Francis," Morrelli said.

Though he carried a broom, the man was dressed in dress slacks, a crisply pressed shirt, tie and long brown cardigan. He looked young despite his dark hair peppered with gray. When he approached them, Maggie noticed he had a slight limp and wore bright white tennis shoes.

"What do you want with Father Francis?"

Before Nick had a chance to say anything, the man seemed to recognize him.

"Wait a minute. I know who you are." He said it as if it were an accusation. "Didn't you play quarterback for the Nebraska Cornhuskers? You're Morrelli, Nick Morrelli."

"You're a Cornhuskers fan?" Morrelli grinned, obviously pleased by the recognition. Maggie noticed dimples. A quarter-back—why wasn't she surprised?

"Big-time fan. My name's Ray…Ray Howard. I just moved back here last spring."

"Glad to meet you. I'm the county sheriff these days. Now, is Father Francis here? It's an official matter."

"I think he's in back changing. He said mass this morning."

"Would you mind getting him for us, Ray?"

Howard disappeared behind the curtain.

Maggie rolled her eyes at Morrelli. "A quarterback, huh?"

"That was a long time ago."

"Were you any good?"

"I had a chance to go on and play for the Dolphins, but my dad insisted on law school."

"Do you always do everything your dad tells you?"

His eyes told her it was a touchy subject. Then he smiled, and said, "Apparently, I do."

"Nicholas." A small gray-haired priest in a black, floor-length cassock had joined them. "Mr. Howard said you had official business to talk to me about."

"Hello, Father Francis. Sorry I didn't call before we dropped in on you."

"That's perfectly all right. You're always welcome here."

"Father, this is Special Agent Maggie O'Dell. She's with the FBI and is here to help me on the Alverez case."

Maggie offered her hand. The old priest took it in both of his.

"It's a pleasure to meet you. Nicholas was an altar boy for me years ago at the old St Margaret's."

"Really?" Maggie glanced at Morrelli, anxious to witness his discomfort. Something behind him caught her eye. The altar curtain moved. There was no breeze, no draft. Then she saw the toes of two white tennis shoes poking out from underneath.

"Father Francis," Nick said, "we wondered if you could answer a few questions."

"Certainly. What can I do to help?"

"I understand you heard Ronald Jeffreys' last confession."

"Yes, but I cannot share any of that with you. I hope you understand."

"Of course we understand," said Maggie. "However, if there is anything that would shed light on the Alverez case, I would hope you'd share it with us."

"The sanctity of confession is to be preserved even for condemned murderers, Agent O'Dell."

"Father," Morrelli said. "There's something else you might be able to help us with. Who, other than a priest, can or is allowed to administer the last rites?"

Father Francis looked confused by the change of subject. "The sacrament of extreme unction should be administered by a priest, but in extreme circumstances it's not necessary."

"Who else would know how?"

"Before Vatican II, it was taught in the Baltimore Catechism. Today, I believe, it is taught only in the seminary, although it may still be a part of some deacon training."

"And what are the requirements for becoming a deacon?" Maggie asked.

"There are rigorous standards. Of course, one must be in good standing with the church. And, unfortunately, only men can be deacons. I'm not sure I understand what any of this has to do with Ronald Jeffreys."

"I'm afraid we can't share that with you, Father." Morrelli smiled. "No disrespect intended." He glanced at Maggie, waiting to see if she had anything more to ask. Then he said, "Thanks for your help, Father Francis."

He motioned to her for them to leave, but she stared at Father Francis, hoping to see something in the hooded eyes that held hers.

"Father Francis," she said, "if you know something… If Jeffreys told you something that could prevent another murder… Father, isn't saving the life of an innocent little boy worth breaking the confidence of a confessed serial killer?"

She waited, staring into those eyes that knew so much more than they were willing or able to reveal.

"What I can tell you is that Ronald Jeffreys told nothing but the truth."

"Excuse me?"

"From the day he confessed to the crime to the day he was executed, Ronald Jeffreys told only the truth. Now, if you'll excuse me."

They stood quietly, watching the priest disappear behind the flowing fabric of the curtains.

"What the hell does that mean?" Morrelli whispered.

"It means we need to take a look at Jeffreys' original confession."

He skidded out of the church parking lot. He needed to calm down. He searched the rearview mirror. No one followed. They had come to the church asking questions. Questions about Jeffreys. They knew nothing. Even that newspaper reporter had insinuated that Danny's murder was a copycat. Someone copycatting Jeffreys. Why hadn't it occurred to any of them that Jeffreys was the copycat? The fact that Jeffreys had also been a cold-blooded murderer had simply made him the perfect patsy.

Within blocks of the school, parents scurried like frightened rats, leading their children, huddling at intersections. They watched them skip up the steps of the school until they were safely inside. Until now, they hardly noticed their children, pretending that "latchkey" was a term of endearment. Leaving them with bruises and scars that, if not stopped, would last a lifetime. And now those same parents were learning. He was actually providing a precious service.

The wind hinted at snow. It reminded him of the blanket in the trunk. Did it still have blood on it? No, he had washed the blanket. There was no blood.

As he drove out of town he noticed a flock of geese overhead getting into formation like fighter pilots from the base.

He turned onto Old Church Road and drove along the river. It wasn't much farther. He pulled off the road into a grove of plum trees. The canopy of branches and leaves hid the car. He shoved the sack of groceries under his arm. He popped the trunk and slung the blanket over his shoulder. He slammed the trunk, its echo bouncing off the trees and water. It was quiet and peaceful despite the wind whispering through the branches, threatening to bring cold.

The muddy leaves hid the wooden door so well that even he had to search for its exact location. He cleared it of all debris, then, with both hands, pulled until it creaked open. A haze of light dimly lit the steps as he descended into the earth, closing the door behind him. As soon as he reached the bottom, he put down the sack and blanket.

From his jacket pocket he pulled the rubber mask. It was better than the ski mask, less frightening and more appropriate for this time of year. Like a zombie, with arms outstretched, he took small steps until he bumped into the wooden shelf-unit. His fingers found the lantern and matches. He struck the match and lit the wick on the first try. The dark came to life in the yellow glow.

He shoved his weight against the thick wooden shelf-unit, using his shoulder to push. The heavy structure groaned, wobbled and began to move. It scraped against the floor, taking clumps of dirt with it. Finally, the secret passage revealed itself. He crawled through the small hole, reaching back to grab the sack and the blanket.

"Jesus," Nick muttered at the line of vehicles parked in front of the Tanner house.

"You have someone here to contain things?" O'Dell asked.

Nick glanced at her beside him in his Jeep.

"I'm only asking, Morrelli. There's no need to get defensive."

She was right. He needed to remember that she was on his side.

The front door of the Tanner house was open. The chatter of voices drifted into the yard. O'Dell knocked on the screen door and waited. Nick would have knocked and entered. Standing so close behind her he noticed she was about six inches shorter than he was. He leaned closer to smell her hair just as a breeze whipped several strands against his chin in a soft caress.

Her fingers brushed her hair back into place, almost grazing his face. He stepped back and watched her tuck the unruly strand behind her ear, revealing soft white skin. This morning she wore a dark burgundy jacket and matching trousers. The color made her skin seem softer, smoother.

The screen door screeched on old hinges as a man Nick didn't recognize opened it just enough to examine the two of them.

"Who are you?" he asked.

"It's okay." Deputy Hal Langston came up behind him and gently nudged the man to the side. Hal opened the screen door. The man shot Hal a look, but walked away.

The Tanner living room was filled with Nick's deputies and with police officers he didn't recognize. Some were drinking coffee, while others huddled over notes and maps. The kitchen was clogged with more bodies.

"Who the fuck are all these people, Hal?"

"It was her idea," Hal whispered. "She called a few neighbors, her mother, the parents of her kid's soccer team."

"Jesus, Hal. We've got the whole team here!"

Nick elbowed his way through the crowd. Then he recognized the woman sitting at the table, sipping coffee with Michelle Tanner.

"What the hell are you doing here?" he bellowed, and the entire room went silent.

Everyone stared as Nick pointed his finger at Christine and said to Michelle Tanner, "Mrs. Tanner, do you realize this woman is a reporter?"

Michelle Tanner was a petite woman, slender to the point of being frail.

"Yes, Sheriff Morrelli. I'm well aware that Christine is a reporter. We think it would be beneficial to have something in tonight's paper…about Matthew."

"Mrs. Tanner, I'm sorry, but I don't think that's a good idea."

"Actually, it's a very good idea."

Christine shifted in her chair, so she could see the woman who appeared from behind Nick. She could have been a model, with flawless skin, lovely high cheekbones, full pouty lips and silky, short dark hair. She carried herself confidently and with an air of authority. Already, Christine liked her.

"Excuse me?" Nick seemed irritated.

"I think it would be a good idea to involve the media right away," said the woman.

"Can I talk to you a minute? Alone." He took the woman's arm, but she immediately jerked it away. Still, she turned to leave the room with him. The crowd opened for her exit. Nick followed.

"Excuse me." Christine patted Michelle's hand. She grabbed her notebook. Despite Nick's fury, she wanted to meet the woman who had just put him in his place. This had to be the FBI expert from Quantico, Special Agent Maggie O'Dell.

Nick and Agent O'Dell huddled in a corner of the living room next to the bay window that overlooked the front yard. Nick was speaking in a hushed tone, confining his anger with clenched teeth. Agent O'Dell looked unscathed by any of it, her voice calm and even.

"Excuse me for interrupting." As she approached Christine felt Nick's glare like a slap in the face. She avoided his eyes. "You must be Special Agent O'Dell. I'm Christine Hamilton." She offered her hand, and O'Dell took it without hesitation.

"Ms. Hamilton."

"In his fury I'm sure Nicky failed to tell you that I'm his sister."

"I wondered if there was a personal connection."

"He's obviously pissed at me, so it's hard for him to see that I'm really here to help."

"I'm sure you are."

"So, you won't mind answering some questions?"

"I'm sorry, Ms. Hamilton…"

"Christine."

"Of course, Christine. Despite my opinions, this isn't my investigation. I'm here strictly to profile this case."

Nick was smiling now.

"So what does that mean? Another press blackout like in the Alverez case?"

"Actually, Christine, I think Sheriff Morrelli has changed his mind," O'Dell said, and Nick's smile transformed into a grimace.

He pushed his hair from his forehead. O'Dell folded her arms over her chest and waited. Christine looked from one to the other. Finally, Nick cleared his throat as though his discomfort was lodged somewhere between larynx and tongue. "There'll be a press conference in the courthouse lobby tomorrow morning at eight-thirty."

"Can I print that in tonight's article?"

"Sure."

"Anything else I can use?"

"No."

"Sheriff Morrelli, didn't you say you already have copies of the boy's photo?" Again, O'Dell said this very matter-of-factly, with no underlying edge. "It may jog some memories if Christine included one with her piece."

He shoved his hands into his pockets, and Christine wondered whether it was so he wouldn't strangle both her and O'Dell.

"Stop by the courthouse and pick one up. I'll instruct Lucy to leave it at the front desk. The front desk, Christine. I don't want you snooping around in my office."

"Relax, Nicky. I keep telling you I'm not the enemy." She started to leave, but turned back at the door. "You're still coming over for dinner tonight, aren't you?"

"I may be too busy."

"Agent O'Dell, would you like to join us? Nothing fancy. I'm fixing spaghetti. There'll be plenty of Chianti."

"Thanks, that sounds nice."

Christine almost burst out laughing at the surprise on Nick's face.

"I'll see the two of you about seven. Nicky knows the address."

The sheriff's department bristled with nervous energy. Nick could feel it as soon as he and O'Dell walked in the door. Phones rang. Machines beeped. Keyboards clicked. Faxes hummed. Radios squawked. Again, there were police officers he didn't recognize and equipment he couldn't identify. He was depending on people he barely knew to handle things he hardly understood. It made him uncomfortable as hell.

"Nick, we've checked every inch of this city." Lloyd Benjamin removed his glasses and wiped his eyes. The oldest member of Nick's team, Lloyd was also the most reliable next to Hal. "Richfield's men are still checking the river where we found the Alverez kid. I've got Staton's men on the north side of town. They're going to check that gravel pit and Northton Lake."

"Good. That's good, Lloyd." Nick patted him on the back. There was something else. Lloyd rubbed his jaw, glanced at O'Dell.

"Some of us were talking," Lloyd continued. "Stan Lubrick thought he remembered Jeffreys having a partner…you know…sort of a…well, a lover, at the time he was arrested. I do remember us bringing a guy in for questioning, but I don't think he ever testified. A Mark Rydell."

"Is it possible to check if Rydell kept in touch with Jeffreys after he was sentenced?" O'Dell asked.

"They may have some information at the penitentiary."

"You might check out what other visitors Jeffreys had or who else he may have kept in touch with. See if there were any prisoners or even guards he befriended."

Nick liked the way her mind processed information. Even Lloyd, who proudly came from a generation dedicated to keeping women in their place, seemed satisfied. He nodded at both of them and went off to find a phone.

"Hey, Nick. That woman called again," Eddie Gillick called out from behind his desk, a phone cradled under his chin.

"Agent O'Dell, here's a fax from Quantico for you." Adam Preston handed her a roll of paper.

"What woman?" Nick asked Eddie.

"Sophie Krichek. Remember, she was the one who said she saw an old blue pickup in the area when the Alverez kid was snatched."

"Let me guess. She saw the pickup again. This time with another little boy who happens to look like Matthew Tanner."

"Wait a minute," O'Dell interrupted, looking up from the trail of fax paper that stretched to the floor. "What makes you think she's not serious?"

"She calls all the time," Nick explained.

"Nick, here's your messages." Lucy handed over a stack of pink "while you were out" slips, and waited in front of him.

"Let me get this straight. You're not going to check out this lead because this woman has surpassed her quota of phone calls?" O'Dell had that look in her eyes that told Nick she thought he was bordering on incompetent.

"Three weeks ago she called to tell us she saw Jesus in her backyard pushing a little girl on a swing. She doesn't even have a backyard. Lucy, are the transcripts from Jeffreys' confession and trial here yet?"

"Max said she'd bring them over herself as soon as possible," Lucy said. "Oh, Agent O'Dell, a Gregory Stewart called for you like three or four times. He said it was important."

"Your boss checking up on you?" Nick said with a smile.

"No, my husband. Is there a phone I can use?"

Nick's smile disappeared. He glanced at her hand. No wedding ring.

"You can use my office," he said. "Down the hall, last door on the right."

"Thanks."

It was ridiculous. This morning at Michelle Tanner's he had been ready to strangle her. Now he felt as if someone had punched him in the stomach.

The office was simple and small with a gray metal desk and matching credenza. Several pictures hung on the wall behind the desk. Maggie sank into the soft leather chair. She picked up the phone while she got a better look at the wall of honor.

There were several photos of young men clad in red and white football jerseys. One photo was obviously a young Morrelli under the sweat and dirt. He stood proudly next to an older gentleman, who, from the scratched autograph, was a Coach Osborne.

In the corner hung two framed degrees. One was from the University of Nebraska. The other was a law degree from…Maggie almost dropped the phone…a law degree from Harvard University. Sheriff Nicholas Morrelli was certainly full of surprises. The more she learned, the more curious she became.

She and Greg had always had a comfortable relationship. Even in the beginning it wasn't so much heat or chemistry that had brought them together, but friendship and common goals. Lately, she wondered if they had drifted apart, or if they had ever been close.

It didn't matter. Marriage was something a person worked at. Greg had called her, made the first move toward reconciliation. That had to be a good sign. She dialed his office and waited patiently through four, five, six rings.

"Brackman, Harvey and Lowe. How may I help you?"

"Greg Stewart, please."

"Mr. Stewart is in a meeting. May I take a message?"

"Could you please see if you can interrupt him? This is his wife. He's been trying to reach me all morning."

"One moment, please."

One moment turned into two, then three. Finally, Greg's voice said, "Maggie, thank God, I got ahold of you. It's your mother. She's in the hospital."

"What was it this time?"

"I think she might be getting serious, Maggie. She used a razor blade."

A little while later Maggie hung up the phone and massaged her temples. She had spent the last twenty minutes arguing with the doctor assigned to her mother's case. He hadn't even looked at her history yet. When Maggie recommended he call her mother's therapist, he sounded relieved, even grateful when she gave him the name and phone number.

They *did* agree that Maggie shouldn't hop on the next plane to Richmond. Her mother was screaming for attention, but Maggie dropping everything and rushing to her side only seemed to reinforce the behavior. Or at least it had the last five times. Dear God, Maggie thought, one of these times her mother would succeed, if only by sheer accident. And although she agreed with Greg that razor blades were a serious advancement, the cuts—according to Dr. Boy Wonder—were horizontal, not vertical.

Maggie sank her throbbing head into the soft leather back of the chair and closed her eyes. She had been taking care of her mother since she was twelve.

There was a soft tap on the office door. Without prompting, the door eased open just enough for Morrelli to peek in.

"O'Dell, you okay in here?"

"I'm fine," she managed to say, but knew immediately that she didn't sound or look very convincing.

His brow furrowed, and soft blue eyes showed concern.

"You look like hell."

"Thanks a lot, Morrelli." But she smiled.

"Listen, could you do me a favor? Call me Nick. Every time you call me Morrelli or Sheriff Morrelli, I start looking around for my dad."

"Okay."

"Lucy is ordering lunch up from Wanda's. What can I get for you? Blue plate special on Monday is meat loaf, but I'd recommend the chicken-fried steak sandwich."

"I'm really not very hungry."

"You need to eat, O'Dell. I'm not going to be responsible for you whittling away that cute little…" He caught himself, but it was too late. The embarrassment washed over his face. He wiped a hand across his jaw as if to erase it. "I'm ordering a ham and cheese sandwich for you." He turned to leave.

"On rye?"

"Okay."

"And with hot mustard?"

Now he smiled, and there were definitely dimples.

"You're a pain in the arse, you know that, O'Dell?"

"Hey, Nick!"

"What now?"

"Call me Maggie."

"Do you like the baseball cards?" The mask muffled his voice.

Matthew stared at him from the small bed in the corner. He sat on top of tangled bedcovers and hugged a pillow to his chest. His eyes were red and puffy. His hair stuck up in places. His soccer uniform was wrinkled. He hadn't even taken off his shoes to sleep last night.

Light filtered in through cracks in the boarded-up window. The wind crept in through the rotted slats. It whistled and howled, creating a ghostly moan and licking at the corners of the posters hiding the cracked walls. The boy hadn't said a word all morning.

"Are you comfortable?" he asked.

When he approached, the boy skittered into the corner, smashing his small body against the crumbling plaster. The chain that connected his ankle to the steel bedpost clanked. There was enough length for the boy to reach the middle of the room. Yet the cheeseburger and fries he had left last night sat untouched on the metal tray. Even the triple-chocolate shake was still filled to the brim.

"Didn't you like your dinner, or do you prefer hot dogs? Maybe even chili dogs? You can have anything you want."

"I wanna go home," Matthew whispered, squeezing the pillow, one hand twisted so he could bite his fingernails. Several were chewed down to the quick and had bled during the night. Dried blood spotted the white cotton pillowcase. It would be hell to wash out.

"Maybe you'd enjoy comic books more than baseball cards. I

have some old Flash Gordons I bet you'd like. I'll bring them with me next time."

He finished unpacking the contents of the grocery sack: three oranges, a bag of Cheetos, two Snickers bars, a six-pack of Hires root beer, two cans of SpaghettiOs and a snack pack of Jell-O chocolate pudding. He laid each item on the old wine crate he had found in what must have been a supply room. He had gone to great lengths to get all of Matthew's favorites.

"It may get chilly tonight," he said as he unrolled the thick wool blanket and draped it over the bed. "I'm sorry I can't leave a light. Is there anything else I can get for you?"

"I wanna go home."

"Your mom doesn't have the time to take care of you, Matthew."

"I want my mom."

"She's never home. And I bet she brings strange men home at night, doesn't she? Ever since she threw your dad out." He kept his voice calm and soothing.

"Please let me go home."

"I'm going to help you, Matthew. I'm going to save you. But you must be patient. Look, I brought all your favorite things."

But still the boy cried, a high-pitched whine that made him grimace. He felt the explosion racing up from his stomach. He must control it. Calm, why couldn't he just remain calm?

"I wanna go home." The wail grated.

"Goddamn it! Shut up, you fucking crybaby."

Christine's article in the evening edition hit downtown Omaha's newsstands at three-thirty. By four o'clock, newspaper carriers tossed the rolled-up *Omaha Journal* onto porches and lawns in Platte City. By four-ten, phones started ringing nonstop in the sheriff's department.

"Nick, Angie Clark has called for you four times." Lucy caught up with him in the hallway, obviously irritated with being the messenger for his love life.

"Next time tell her I'm sorry, but I just don't have time to talk."

She started to walk away, but spun back.

"Oh, I almost forgot. Max is on her way down the hall with those transcripts from Jeffreys' confession and trial."

"Great. Tell Agent O'Dell, would you, please?"

"Where do you want me to put them?" She skipped alongside him as he made his way to his office.

"Can't you just give them to Agent O'Dell?"

"All five boxes?"

"Five boxes?"

"You know Max. She's pretty thorough, so everything's labeled and cataloged. She said to tell you she also included copies of all the evidence that was entered and logged, as well as affidavits from witnesses who didn't testify."

"Five boxes?" He shook his head. "Put them in my office."

"Okay." She turned to leave, then stopped again. "Do you still want me to tell Agent O'Dell?"

"Yes, please."

"Oh, and the mayor's holding on line three for you."

"Lucy, we can't afford to hold up any of those lines."

"I know, but he insisted. I couldn't just hang up on him."

Yes, he was sure Brian Rutledge would have insisted. He was a royal pain in the ass.

Nick retreated to his office. He grabbed the phone and punched line three.

"Hi, Brian. It's Nick."

"Nick, what the hell's going on over there? I've been on hold for goddamn near twenty minutes."

"Don't mean to inconvenience you, Brian. We're a little busy."

"I've got a crisis of my own, Nick. City council thinks I should cancel Halloween. Goddamn it, Nick, I cancel Halloween and I look like the goddamn Grinch."

"I think the Grinch is Christmas, Brian."

"Goddamn it, Nick. This isn't funny."

"I'm not laughing, Brian. But you know what? I have a few more serious things to worry about than Halloween."

Lucy peeked in from behind his door. He waved her in. She opened the door and motioned for the four men following her to set the boxes in the corner under the window.

"Halloween is serious, Nick. What if this nut ends up pulling something when all those kids are out running around in the dark?"

"Brian, what do you want from me?"

"I want to know how goddamn serious this thing is. Do you have any suspects? Are you making any arrests in the near future? What the hell are you doing over there?"

"One boy is dead and another is missing. How goddamn serious do you think this is, Brian? As far as how I handle the investigation, it's none of your fucking business. We need this phone line open for more important things than reassuring your sorry ass, so don't call again." He slammed the phone down and noticed O'Dell standing in the doorway, watching him.

"Lucy told me the transcripts were in here."

"They are. Come on in. Close the door behind you. The boxes are here under the window."

Within a very short time O'Dell was on her knees. She had several box lids off and files scattered on the floor around her.

"Can I get you a chair?"

"No, thanks. It'll be easier this way."

She looked as though she had found what she was looking for. She opened the file and began scanning the contents, flipping pages, then settling on one. Suddenly, her entire face went serious. Her eyes darted over the page. She sat back on her feet.

"What is it?"

"It's Jeffreys' original confession, right after his arrest."

"Okay, and Father Francis said Jeffreys hadn't lied. That means the details are true. So what?"

"Did you realize that Jeffreys confessed to murdering only Bobby Wilson? In fact," she said, flipping through several more pages, "in fact, he was adamant about having nothing to do with the other two boys' murders."

"I don't remember hearing any of that. They probably thought he was lying."

"But if he wasn't?"

"Okay, if he wasn't lying, and he did kill only Bobby Wilson…" Nick didn't finish. Suddenly, he felt sick to his stomach, even before Maggie finished his sentence:

"Then the real serial killer got away, and he's back."

Christine hoped Nick didn't detect the relief in her voice when he called to cancel dinner. If this new lead panned out, she'd be working late to claim yet another front page on tomorrow morning's paper.

"Can we do it tomorrow night?" he asked.

"Sure, no problem."

She turned the corner into the parking lot as she flipped her cellular phone closed and shoved it into her purse. Nick would be furious if he knew where she was.

Inside the main entrance a heavy metal trash can held open the security door. It overflowed with cigarette butts. Christine stepped carefully.

Apartment 410 was on the fourth floor, at the end of the hallway. A hand-braided welcome mat lay outside the scratched and battered door. The mat was clean, spotless.

Christine knocked and held her breath to avoid the hallway's suffocating odors. Several locks clicked inside, then the door opened just a crack. A pair of hooded and wrinkled blue eyes peered at her through thick glasses.

"Mrs. Krichek?"

"Are you that reporter?"

"Yes. Yes, I am. My name is Christine Hamilton."

The door opened, and she waited for the woman to back out of the way with her walker. The apartment smelled much cleaner than the hallway. Colorful afghans and quilts were draped over the couch and a rocker. Green plants hung above the windows.

"Sit," the old woman instructed, backing herself into the rocker. Her brilliant blue eyes were magnified and distorted by the thick wire-rimmed glasses. Her white hair was twisted neatly into a bun, clasped by beautiful turquoise hair combs.

Christine said, "I'd like to get right to what you saw the morning Danny Alverez disappeared. You don't mind, do you?"

"No. Not at all. I'm glad somebody's finally interested."

"The sheriff's office has never come here to question you?"

"I called them twice. In fact, just this morning before I seen your article. They hemmed and hawed like they think I'm making it up or something. So, then I called you. I don't care what anybody says, I seen what I seen."

"And just what did you see, Mrs. Krichek?"

"I seen that boy park his bike and get in an old blue pickup."

"Are you sure it was the Alverez boy?"

"Seen him dozens of times. He was a good little paperboy. Brought my newspaper all the way to my door and laid it on my mat. Not like the kid we have now. He steps off the elevator and tosses it down here. Sometimes it makes it. Sometimes it doesn't. I think your paper should make sure those kids do a better job."

"I'll let them know, Mrs. Krichek. Tell me about the pickup. Could you see the driver?"

"No. It was still dark out. I stood right at that there window. Sun was barely coming up. He pulled into the parking lot so that the passenger's side was all I could see. He must've said something to the boy, 'cause Danny leaned his bike against the fence, came around and got up into the pickup."

"Danny got into the pickup? Are you sure the man didn't grab him and pull him in?"

"No, no. It was all quite friendly—otherwise I would have called the sheriff sooner. It wasn't until I heard Danny was missing that I put two and two together."

Christine stood and went to the window the woman had pointed to. Below was a perfect view of the parking lot and the chain-link fence. Even someone with poor vision could make out the events Mrs. Krichek had described.

"What kind of pickup?"

"I know little about cars and trucks." The woman hoisted herself back into the walker and shuffled over to join Christine. "It was old, royal blue with paint chipped and some rust. You know, on the bottom part. It had running boards. I remember 'cause Danny stepped up on it to climb in. And it had wooden stockracks, homemade ones on the back. The kind farmers put on when they're hauling something. Oh, and one of the headlights wasn't working."

Christine jotted down the details. "Were you able to see any of the license plate?"

"No, my eyes aren't that good."

A screen door slammed below, and a little girl raced out into a backyard on the other side of the fence. She jumped onto a swing. The man who followed had long hair and a beard and wore blue jeans with a long tunic-like shirt.

"They just moved in last month." Mrs. Krichek nodded down at the pair as the man pushed the little girl on the swing, and she squealed with delight. "The first day I saw him, I tell you I thought I was looking down at the Lord himself. Don't you think he looks like Jesus?"

Christine smiled and nodded.

Maggie watched Nick step carefully around the piles of documents she had scattered all over the floor of his office. He cleared a spot and set down the steaming pizza and cold Pepsis. Then he joined her on the floor, his long legs stretching out next to her.

She had removed her shoes hours ago and had sat on her feet until they fell asleep. Now she massaged them one at a time while she read the coroner's reports on Aaron Harper and Eric Paltrow, the two dead boys whom Jeffreys may have erroneously been convicted of killing.

The pizza smelled good despite the gruesome details she read. She glanced up to find Nick watching her rub her feet. Immediately, he looked away as though she had caught him at something. He popped open a can of Pepsi and handed it to her.

"Thanks."

Nick lifted a thick slice of pizza, pulling it expertly away so he didn't lose the cheese. He plopped it down onto a paper plate and handed it to Maggie. She could smell green peppers, Italian sausage and Romano cheese. He had done good. She bit off more than she should have, dripping cheese and sauce down her chin.

"Jesus, O'Dell, you've got sauce all over your face."

She licked the side of her mouth.

"Other side." He pointed. "And on your chin."

Her hands were full of pizza and coroner reports. She licked at the other side.

"No, higher. Here, let me."

As soon as his thumb touched the corner of her mouth, her eyes met his. His fingers wiped at her chin. His thumb rolled over her lower lip where she was certain there was no sauce or cheese. In his eyes she saw that he felt the unexpected surge of electricity, too. His fingertips lingered longer than necessary on her chin, moved up, caressed her cheek. His thumb took its time to leave her lip and wipe the corner of her mouth. Completely surprised by her body's reaction, she shifted away, just out of his reach.

"Thanks," she managed to say, now avoiding his eyes. She put down the pizza, grabbed a napkin and finished the job, rubbing harder than necessary in an attempt to wipe away the electrical current.

"I think we might need more napkins and Pepsis."

Nick scrambled to his feet. Maggie looked up at him; he seemed flustered. So the touch, the caress, had caught him off guard, too.

"There are so many discrepancies," she said, trying to get her mind back on the coroner's reports. "I don't know why anyone believed Jeffreys killed all three boys."

"But don't serial killers change the way they do things?"

"What's unusual here is that the Harper and Paltrow murders were almost identical. Both were bound, hands behind their backs, with rope. They were strangled and their throats slashed. The chest wounds resembled each other almost exactly down to the number of puncture wounds. The same knife was used to carve the Xs. Neither boy appeared to have been sexually molested. Their bodies were found in different remote areas near the river. The Wilson boy, on the other hand—"

"I know," Nick interrupted. "His hands were bound in front with duct tape, no rope. He was stabbed to death—no signs of strangulation. His throat wasn't slashed. A hunting knife was used. Though there were plenty of puncture wounds…"

"Twenty-two."

"Twenty-two puncture wounds, but no carving."

"The Wilson boy was also sodomized, repeatedly," Maggie added.

"And his body was found in a park Dumpster, instead of by the river." Nick grabbed his Pepsi and emptied the can, wiping his mouth with the back of his hand. "Okay, there's a lot of differences, but couldn't Jeffreys have changed things? Even the sodomy, couldn't that be seen as…I don't know…an escalation?"

"Yes, it could," she agreed. "But remember the sequence was Harper, Wilson, Paltrow. It would be very unusual for a killer to change, to experiment, to escalate and then go back to the exact original format. He uses one knife—something with a small blade—perhaps a fillet knife. Then he changes to a hunting knife, then back to the other knife. Even the styles are very different. The Harper and Paltrow murders are meticulous in detail. Both boys were murdered by someone taking his time—someone who enjoys inflicting pain. Very much like Danny Alverez's murder. Bobby Wilson's murder, however, looks like it was done in the heat of the moment with too much emotion and passion to pay any attention to detail."

"You know, I always thought it seemed too easy," Nick said wearily. "I've been wondering if my dad wasn't so caught up in the media circus that he may have overlooked something."

"What do you mean?"

"Don't get me wrong. I'm not saying my dad would purposely jeopardize any case. I'm just saying that it all seemed a bit too easy—the way my dad caught Jeffreys. One day there was an anonymous tip, and the next day they had Jeffreys babbling out a confession."

"What kind of anonymous tip?"

"It was a phone call, I think. I don't know for sure. I wasn't living here at the time. I was teaching down at UNL, so I got most of this stuff secondhand. Isn't there anything in the reports?"

Maggie searched through several file folders. "I haven't seen anything at all about an anonymous tip," she said, handing him the file labeled "Jeffreys' Arrest". "What do you remember? Your father's reports are very detailed, including a blow-by-blow of the actual arrest. He even includes the evidence they found in the trunk of Jeffreys' Chevy Impala." She checked her own notes and read the list. "They found a roll of duct tape, a hunting knife, some rope…wait a minute."

She stopped to check that she had copied the list correctly. "A pair of boy's underpants, which were later identified as belonging to…" She looked up at Nick, who had found the list in the report and was reading the same items she had in front of her. His eyes met hers, revealing he was thinking precisely what she was.

She continued, "A pair of underpants later identified as Eric Paltrow's."

Maggie rifled through the coroner's report to double-check her memory, though she already knew what she would find. "Eric Paltrow's body was found with his underpants on."

They stared at each other, neither wanting to acknowledge out loud what they had stumbled upon. Ronald Jeffreys had been framed for two murders he hadn't committed, and there was a good chance the frame-up had been done by someone in the sheriff's department.

Tuesday, October 28

The press conference had turned into a lynch mob within minutes, especially after Christine's morning headline: SHERIFF'S DEPARTMENT IGNORES LEADS IN ALVEREZ CASE.

Nick thought for sure Eddie had checked out where old lady Krichek lived, after her first call. Why the hell wouldn't he have realized Krichek had a perfect view of the parking lot where Danny had been abducted? Jesus, he wanted to strangle Eddie or, worse, offer him up to the media as a scapegoat. Instead, he let him off with a simple and private verbal lashing and a warning. Hell, right now he needed every officer he had. It was no time to be losing his cool, which he almost did at the press conference when the questions got ugly.

But O'Dell, in her calm and authoritative manner, had rapidly put things back in perspective. She had challenged the media to help find the mysterious blue pickup, making them a part of the hunt for the killer instead of hunting for faults in the sheriff's department. He began wondering what he'd do without her and hoped he wouldn't have to find out any time soon.

He turned the Jeep onto Christine's street. It had gotten colder with a biting wind promising the temperature would drop even more.

Maggie had spent the entire trip beside him, buried in the Alverez file. Photos were spread across her lap. Since Matthew Tanner's disappearance, a hundred and seventy-five deputies, police officers and independent investigators had been searching almost nonstop. Not one shred of evidence brought them closer to finding the boy. It really did seem as though someone had pulled up alongside Matthew and had him willingly get into his vehicle, just as Sophie Krichek had described in the case of the Alverez boy.

If that was true, then there was a good chance the killer was someone the boys knew and trusted. Jesus, Nick would rather believe the boys were disappearing into thin air than being killed and mutilated by someone they knew.

Nick absently pulled into the driveway and hit the brakes, sending photos across the seat and onto the floor.

"Sorry." He shoved the Jeep into park, and reached across to pick up the photos. Their arms criss-crossed each other. Their foreheads brushed. He handed her the photos he had retrieved, and she thanked him without looking at him. They had been tiptoeing around each other all day. He wasn't sure if it was to avoid talking about their discovery in the Jeffreys case or to avoid touching one another.

At Christine's door, Maggie's cellular phone began ringing.

"Agent Maggie O'Dell."

Christine motioned for them to come in. "I thought for sure you'd cancel," she whispered to Nick and led him to the living room, leaving Maggie to the privacy of the foyer.

"Because of the article?"

"No, because you're swamped. You're not mad about the article, are you?"

"Krichek is nutty as a fruitcake. I doubt she saw anything."

"She's convincing, Nicky. There's nothing wrong with the lady. You should be looking for an old blue pickup."

Nick eyed Maggie. He could see her pacing. He wished he could hear her conversation. Then, suddenly, he got his wish as her angry voice carried into the living room.

"Go to hell, Greg!" She snapped the phone shut and shoved it into her pocket.

"Who's Greg?"

"Her husband."

"I didn't know she was married."

"Why wouldn't she be?"

Maggie came in.

"Sorry about that. Lately, my husband has had the annoying tendency of pissing me off."

"That's why I got rid of mine," Christine said with a smile. "Nicky, get Maggie some wine. I need to check up on dinner." She patted Maggie on the shoulder on her way out.

The wine and glasses were on the coffee table in front of him. Nick poured, Maggie paced, obviously distracted. She stopped at the window and stared out into the backyard. He picked up the glasses and came alongside her.

"You okay?" He handed her the wine.

"Have you ever been married, Nick?"

"No, I've done a pretty good job avoiding it."

They stood quietly, side by side.

He said, "I couldn't help noticing you don't wear a wedding ring."

"It's at the bottom of the Charles River."

"Excuse me?"

"About a year ago, we were dragging a floater from the river."

"A floater?"

"A body that's been in the water a while. The water was very cold. My ring must have slipped off."

"You never replaced it?"

"No. I think maybe subconsciously I realized all those things it was supposed to symbolize were long gone."

"Uncle Nick!" Timmy interrupted, running into the room and jumping up into Nick's arms. Nick spiraled him around, hugging him close while Timmy's little legs threatened to knock down the knickknacks scattered about.

"You guys!" Christine yelled from the doorway. Then to Maggie, "It's like having two kids in the house."

Nick set Timmy down.

"Maggie, this is my son, Timmy," said Christine. "Timmy, this is Special Agent Maggie O'Dell."

"So you're an FBI agent just like Agent Mulder and Agent Scully on *The X-Files*?"

"Except I don't track aliens. Although some of the people I track down are pretty scary."

"I have some *X-Files* posters in my bedroom. Would you like to see them?"

"Do we have time?" Maggie asked Christine.

Timmy waited for his mom's "Sure." Then he grabbed Maggie's hand and led her down the hall.

The small room was wonderfully cluttered. A baseball mitt hung on the bedpost. A *Jurassic Park* bedspread covered lumps she guessed were matching pajamas. On a corner bookshelf, an old microscope propped up copies of *King Arthur, Galaxy of the Stars* and *The Collector's Encyclopedia of Baseball Cards.* The walls were hidden, plastered with an odd assortment of posters.

Timmy led Maggie to the dresser. He pointed to the empty hull of a horseshoe crab. "My grandpa brought this home for me from Florida. He and Grandma travel a lot. You can touch it if you want."

She ran her finger over the smooth shell. She noticed a photo behind the crab. About two dozen boys in matching T-shirts and shorts lined the inside of a canoe and the dock behind it. She recognized the boy at the front of the canoe and leaned in for a closer view. Her pulse quickened. She lifted the photo, careful not to disturb the crab. The boy was Danny Alverez.

"What's this photo, Timmy?"

"Oh, that's church camp. My mom made me go. I thought it'd ruin my summer, but it was fun."

"Isn't this boy Danny Alverez?"

"Yeah, that's him."

"So you knew him?"

"Not really. He was down in the Red Robin cabins. I was in the Goldenrod."

"Didn't he go to your church?"

"No, I think he went to school and church out by the air force base. Do you want to see my baseball card collection?"

"How many boys were there at camp?"

"I don't know. Lots."

There were two adults in the photo. One was Ray Howard, the janitor from St Margaret's. The other was a tall, handsome man with dark curly hair and a boyish face. Both he and Howard wore gray T-shirts with St Margaret's written across the front.

"Timmy, who's this guy in the photo?"

"Oh, that's Father Keller. He's really cool. I'm one of his altar boys this year. Not many boys get to be his altar boys. He's really choosy."

"How is he choosy?"

"Just by making sure they're reliable and stuff. He treats us special, sort of like our reward for being good altar boys."

"How does he treat you special?"

"He's taking us camping this Thursday and Friday. And sometimes he plays football with us. Oh, and he trades baseball cards. Once I traded him a Bob Gibson for a Joe DiMaggio."

Another face caught her eye. Up on the dock, partially hidden behind a bigger boy, peered the small, freckled face of Matthew Tanner.

"Timmy, do you mind if I borrow this photo for a few days?"

"Okay."

"Timmy." Christine was at the door. "It's time for dinner. You need to wash up." She held the door open and swatted him with a kitchen towel on his way out.

Maggie slipped the photo into her jacket pocket without Christine noticing.

After dinner Nick insisted he and Timmy do the dishes. Christine knew it was all for Maggie's benefit, but she decided to take advantage of her little brother's temporary generosity.

The two women retreated to the living room where they heard only the muffled discussion of Nebraska football. Christine set the coffee cups and saucers on the glass tabletop and wished Maggie would sit down and relax. Stop being Agent O'Dell for a few minutes. She'd seemed restless throughout dinner and was now pacing. Her body seemed wired with energy, though she looked exhausted. The puffy eyes were poorly concealed with makeup. She was easily distracted.

"Come, sit," Christine finally said, patting the spot on the sofa next to her. "I thought I couldn't keep still, but I think you've got me beaten."

"Sorry. Maybe I've been spending too much time with killers and dead bodies. My manners seem to have disappeared."

"Nonsense. You've just been spending too much time with Nicky."

Maggie smiled. "Dinner was delicious. It's been a long time since I've had a home-cooked meal."

"Thanks, but I've had lots of practice. I was a stay-at-home mom until my husband decided he liked twenty-three-year-old receptionists."

The phone rang. Christine crossed the room and picked up before its third ring.

"Hello?"

"Christine, it's Hal. Sorry to bother you. Is Nick still there?" His voice crackled. She heard humming, an engine. He was in his car.

"Yes. As a matter of fact, he is."

She put the phone down and called out, "Nick, it's Hal. For you."

Before she could say anything more, Nick was at her side, reaching for the phone.

"Hal, what is it?" He turned his back to them and listened. "Don't let anyone touch anything." The panic in his voice exploded, laced with urgency. "I mean it, Hal." Now there was anger to camouflage the panic. It didn't fool Christine. She knew her brother all too well. "Secure the area, but don't let anyone touch a thing. O'Dell's here with me. We'll be there in about fifteen to twenty minutes." When he turned, his eyes immediately sought out Maggie's as he hung up the phone.

"My God. They found Matthew's body, didn't they?" Christine said what only seemed obvious.

"Christine, I swear, if you print a word…" The angry panic threatened to turn into fury.

"People have the right to know."

"Not before his mother. Will you, at least, please have the decency to wait—for her sake?"

"On one condition…"

"Jesus, Christine, listen to yourself!"

"Just promise you'll call me when it's okay to go ahead. Is that too much to ask?"

Christine waited until the Jeep's taillights turned the corner at the end of the street. She grabbed the phone and punched *69. It rang only once.

"Deputy Langston," said a voice.

"Hal, hi, it's Christine." Before he could ask any questions she hurried on. "Nicky and Maggie just left. Nicky asked me to keep trying George Tillie. You know old George, he could sleep through World War III."

"Yeah?"

"I can't remember the exact location, you know, to tell George."

Silence. Damn, he was onto her.

She took a stab. "It's off Old Church Road..."

"Right." He sounded relieved. "Tell George to go a mile past the state-park marker. He can leave his car in Ron Woodson's pasture, up on top of the hill. He'll see the spotlights down in the woods. We'll be close to the river."

"Thanks, Hal. I keep hoping it's some runaway and not Matthew, for Michelle's sake."

"I know what you mean. But there's no doubt. It's Matthew. I gotta go. Tell George to be careful walking down there."

She waited for the click, then dialed Taylor Corby's home number.

Light snow glittered in the Jeep's headlights. They parked on an incline that overlooked the river. Spotlights illuminated the grove of trees below, creating eerie shadows, ghosts with spindly arms that waved in the breeze.

The temperature had plunged in the last two hours. Within seconds, snowflakes clung to Maggie's eyelashes, her hair and her clothes. To make matters worse, they had over a quarter of a mile to walk. The underbrush was thick—like walking through knee-deep water. A narrow path twisted through the trees. Nick led the way, snapping branches and twigs. Those that escaped his grasp whipped Maggie's face.

The path ended at the river's bank, where a line of cattails and tall grass separated the woods from the water. Hal met them. He led the way while Nick threw questions at him, receiving only nods as answers.

"Bob Weston is sending an FBI forensic team to collect evidence. Nobody else gets through. Nobody. You got that, Hal?"

Suddenly, Hal stopped and pointed. At first, Maggie saw nothing. Snowflakes danced like fireflies in the harsh light of the spotlights. Then she saw him, the little white body with a necklace of blood, naked in the snow-laced grass. His chest was so small, the jagged X slashed from his neck to his waist. His arms lay by his sides, his fists clenched. There had been no need to tie this boy who was much too small to present any threat to his killer.

She left both men and approached slowly. Yes, the body had

been washed clean. She knelt beside him and carefully brushed the snow from his forehead. She saw the smudge of oily liquid. It also smeared his blue lips and left another smudge between the X over his heart.

He had been out here for a while. Even the sudden cold couldn't disguise the smell. She noticed small puncture marks on the inside of his left thigh, deep but leaving no trace of blood. They had been made after the boy was dead. Perhaps an animal, she thought as she dug out a small flashlight. The punctures were definitely teeth, but human teeth, she realized, overlapping several times as though bitten in a madness or purposely to disguise the imprint. They were close to the groin, but she couldn't see any marks on the penis. He hadn't done this before. The killer was adding to his routine.

Suddenly she noticed it. A torn piece of paper peeked from between the tiny fingers. Matthew Tanner had something clutched tightly in his fist. She glanced over her shoulder. Nick and Hal stood where she had left them. Their backs were turned to her as they watched five men in FBI windbreakers descend the wooded ridge.

As gently as possible, she twisted the fingers, now stiff and unbending in the advance stages of rigor mortis. She dislodged the crumpled piece of paper. It was thicker than paper and no more than a torn corner. Without even examining it closely, she recognized what it was. Twisted tightly in Matthew Tanner's fist was the corner of a baseball card.

The forensic team worked quickly, now threatened by a new enemy. Snow fell more heavily, covering leaves and branches, burying valuable evidence.

Maggie and Nick were huddled near the tree line, out of the wind's merciless path. Maggie couldn't believe how cold it had become.

"Do you want me to go with you to Michelle Tanner's?"

He hesitated. "I'd like to wait until morning, not just because I don't want to wake her up in the middle of the night. It might be a while before they get him to the morgue. And no matter how painful it is, she'll want to see him."

"That certainly makes sense. In the morning she may have more people there to lean on. And you're right. By the time they get finished here, it will be morning."

"I'll let these guys know we're leaving."

He had started for the forensic team when Maggie saw something and grabbed his arm. Not more than fifteen feet behind Nick was a set of footprints—bare footprints, freshly stamped in the snow.

"Nick, wait," she whispered. "He's here."

"What are you talking about?"

"The killer. He's here."

"Do you see him?"

"No, but he's here."

"O'Dell, I think the cold has frozen your brain."

"Directly behind you, next to that tree with the huge knot. There's a set of footprints, bare footprints made in the snow."

She loosened her grip, allowing him to look.

"Jesus!" His eyes darted around before they made their way back to hers. "With the snow falling as heavy as it is, those were made recently, very recently. Like, say, minutes ago. The son of a bitch may have been right behind us. What the hell do we do?"

"You stay here. Wait for Hal. I'll head up the path like I'm going back to the cars. From up above I might be able to see him."

"I'll come with you."

"No, he'll notice if he's watching. Wait for Hal. I'll need the two of you as backup. Stay calm and try not to look around."

He was here. He was watching. She could feel it. Was this part of his ritual? She started up the path. Her leather flats were caked with snow. She grabbed at branches, tree roots and vines. Within minutes she was out of breath.

A branch snapped off in her hands, sending her skidding. She slammed to a stop, ramming her hip into a tree. She crawled back to her feet. She was almost to the police perimeter. She could hear the crime-scene tape flapping in the wind. Just above her, she heard voices.

The ground finally leveled enough for her to stand without assistance. She veered off the path and headed into the thick brush. From above she could see Nick at the bottom of the tree line. Hal was just joining him. Between the trees and the river, the forensic team worked quickly, hunching over the small body and filling little plastic bags of evidence.

Below her, something moved in the trees. Maggie froze. She listened. Had she imagined seeing movement?

A twig snapped not more than a hundred feet below. Then she saw him. He was pressed against a tree. In the shadows of the spotlights he looked like an extension of the bark. He blended in, tall, thin and black from head to bare feet. She had been right. He was watching the forensic team below. He started moving from tree to tree, smooth and sleek like an animal. He was leaving.

Maggie pulled out her gun. She followed, not letting him out of her sight. Twigs scratched her face and grabbed her hair. Branches stabbed at her legs.

Now they were on level ground, just on the edge of the woods.

He was making his way to the perimeter, using the trees to camouflage himself. Suddenly, he stopped and looked back. She scrambled behind a tree. Had he seen her? She hoped the pounding of her heart didn't betray her. The wind whirled around her, a ghostly moan. The river was close enough for her to hear its rolling water.

She peered out from behind the tree. She couldn't see him. He was gone. There was only silence ahead. Silence and darkness, well beyond the spotlight's reach now.

It had only been seconds. He couldn't be gone. She slid around the tree and strained to see into the darkness. She walked slowly and carefully, keeping close to the trees. There was nothing separating the woods from the steep riverbank, a ridge of three to four feet that the water had carved out. Below, the water was black and fast-moving.

Suddenly, she heard a twig snap. She heard him running—legs swishing through grass—before she could see him. She spun to her right where branches cracked. An explosion of sound came at her. She turned and fired a warning shot into the air just as he emerged from the thicket, a huge, black shadow, charging straight for her. She aimed, but before she had time to squeeze the trigger, he knocked into her, sending her backward, flying through the air and plunging the two of them into the river.

The cold water stung her body like thousands of snakebites. She clung to her gun and raised her arm to fire at the floating black mass only feet away from her. Pain shot through her shoulder. She twisted and tried again. This time she felt metal stabbing into her flesh. It was only then she realized she had crashed into a pile of debris. It held her from being washed away by the current. And something was ripping into her shoulder. She tried to break free, but it only stabbed deeper and tore into her flesh.

She heard the voices above yelling to each other. The stampede of footsteps ground to a halt, and a half-dozen flashlights came over the edge, blinding her. In the new light she twisted again, despite the pain. But there was nothing on the river's surface for as far as she could see. He was gone.

The frigid water paralyzed his body. His muscles screamed with pain. His lungs threatened to burst. He held his breath and kept his body submerged. The river carried him. He didn't fight its power, its rapid force. Instead, he allowed it to rescue him once again.

They were close. So close he could see the flitters of flashlights dance across the surface. To his right. To his left. Just above his head. Voices yelled to each other.

No one dived in after him. No one except for Special Agent O'Dell, who wasn't going anywhere. She had entangled herself neatly into the little present he had found for her. The bitch had gotten what she deserved.

The river carried him downstream. He sneaked to the surface for air. He smiled. Special Agent O'Dell would hate being rescued. First being incapacitated and helpless and now being rescued. Would it shock her to discover how much he knew about her? Did she really expect to dig inside his mind and not have him return the gesture? Finally, a worthy adversary to keep him on his toes, unlike these small-town hicks.

Something floated next to him, small and black. He grabbed the hard plastic. It flipped open and a light flashed on. It was a cellular phone. What a shame to see it go to waste. He stuffed it into the pocket of his pants.

He maneuvered himself closer to the riverbank. In seconds, he found his marker. He grabbed the crooked branch that hung over the water. It creaked under his weight, but didn't break.

The current pushed and slapped against his body. The water possessed a strength, a power that demanded respect. He understood that, welcomed it and used it to his advantage.

His fingers stung with cold as he clawed his way along the branch. His arms ached. Only another foot, a few more inches. His feet struck land, ice-cold, snow-covered land. He ran through the ice-coated sea of grass. He gasped for breath but didn't slow his pace.

He found his hiding spot. The grove of plum trees sagged with snow-covered branches, adding a cave-like effect to the already thick canopy. Just then, a sudden ringing sent him into a frenzy. Quickly, he realized it was the phone. He dug it out, held it for two, three rings, staring at it. Finally, he flipped it open. It lit up again. The ringing stopped.

Someone was yelling, "Hello!"

"Hello?"

"Is this Maggie O'Dell's phone?"

"Yes, it is. She dropped it."

"Can I talk to her?"

"She's kind of tied up right now."

"Well, tell her that her husband, Greg, called, and that her mother is in serious shape. She needs to call the hospital. You got that?"

"Sure."

He peeled off the black sweatpants, sweatshirt and ski mask, wiped himself down and pulled on dry jeans and a thick wool sweater.

He sat on the running board to tie his tennis shoes, then climbed up into the old pickup. The engine sputtered to life, and he drove home, shivering and squinting as the one headlight cut through the night.

It had seemed like a good idea at the time. His house was less than a mile away. She had been soaked to the bone and bleeding. Now Nick wasn't so sure he should have brought her here.

He had left her in the master bathroom upstairs. He had taken a shower downstairs, lit a fire in the fireplace and hung her clothes to dry in the utility room. From the sound of running water in the pipes above him, he knew she was still in the shower.

The medicine cabinet in the utility room was well stocked. He filled his arms with cotton balls, rubbing alcohol, gauze, washcloths, hydrogen peroxide and a tin of salve. He set up his nursing station by the fire, adding pillows and blankets.

He turned to find her coming down the staircase. She wore his old terry-cloth robe. It parted with every step, just enough to reveal well-shaped calves, sometimes a glimpse of a firm, smooth thigh. No, there would be absolutely nothing simple about this.

As soon as she saw his arsenal of healing tools, she shook her head. "I think I washed everything out. None of that is necessary."

"It's either this or I take you to the hospital."

She frowned at him.

"Humor me, okay? That wire was full of rust. When was your last tetanus shot?"

"I'm sure it's up-to-date. The Bureau hauls us in every three years, whether we need it or not. Look, Morrelli, I appreciate the gesture, but I really am fine."

He uncapped the alcohol and peroxide, lined up cotton balls and pointed to the ottoman in front of him. "Sit!"

Perhaps she was too tired to argue. She sat down, loosened the robe's cinch, and let it drop off her shoulder while she held it tightly at her breasts.

Immediately, he found himself distracted by her smooth, creamy skin, the swell of her breasts, the curve of her neck, the fresh scent of her hair and skin. He felt light-headed, and already he was hard. How could he touch her and not want to do more? It was stupid. He needed to concentrate and ignore his erection for once in his life.

About a half-dozen bloody, triangular marks marred her beautiful skin, starting on top of her shoulder and trailing down her shoulder blade and arm. Several were deep and bleeding.

He dabbed an alcohol-soaked cotton ball against the first puncture, and she jerked from the sting. However, she made no sound.

"Are you okay?"

"Fine."

He cleaned each wound, hoping the alcohol would sterilize as much as it stung. Then he applied gauze and tape to those that kept bleeding.

Finally finished, he ran his open palm over the top of her shoulder and continued the slow caress down her arm, letting his hand make the journey he wished his mouth could. He felt her tremble, just slightly. Her back straightened, alerting her body to danger or responding to the electricity. His hand lingered, enjoying the sensation of silky skin. Then gently, reluctantly, he lifted the robe up over her shoulder. She tightened the cinch.

"Thanks," she said.

"Can I get you anything…hot chocolate, brandy?"

"Brandy would be nice." She left the ottoman and sat on the rug in front of the fireplace, leaning against a pile of pillows and tucking the robe in around her shapely legs.

"Can I fix you some soup, maybe a sandwich?"

She smiled up at him. "Why is it that you're always trying to feed me, Morrelli?"

"Probably because I'm not allowed to do the things I'd really like to do with you."

The color rose in her cheeks. He was bordering on totally inappropriate behavior. Yet all he could think about was whether she felt as hot as he did. Finally, she looked away, and he retreated to the kitchen while he was still able to move.

The photo Maggie had retrieved from her jacket pocket was creased and wrinkled. The corners curled as it dried. She owed Timmy a replacement, though she didn't know how she'd accomplish that. At least the photo hadn't disappeared into the dark water like her cell phone.

Nick was taking a long time in the kitchen. She wondered whether he had decided on a sandwich, after all. The entire time he dressed her wounds, she welcomed the sting of pain. It was the only thing that kept her mind from relishing his touch. When he finished by running his hand over her shoulder and down her arm, she was shocked to find herself waiting breathlessly, hoping for the caress to continue. Now, she wondered what it would feel like to have his big, steady hands caressing her neck, sliding gently over her shoulders and slowly down to her breasts.

She heard Nick come into the room and her hand flew to her face. Her skin was flushed again, but the fire would account for that. She steadied herself and avoided looking up at him as he approached.

He handed her a glass of brandy, then sat next to her. He pulled his long, bare feet up underneath himself, leaning so close he brushed her shoulder.

"So, that's the photo you told me about?" He grabbed a handmade quilt off the sofa. He began wrapping it around their legs. He did this as though it was natural for the two of them to be curling up next to each other. The intimacy of the act immediately sent the heat from her face down to other parts of her body.

She handed him the photo. With both hands now cupped around the globe of brandy, she swirled the liquid in the glass, breathed in its sweet, stout aroma, then took a sip. She closed her eyes, tilted her head back against the soft pillows and enjoyed the lovely sting sliding down her throat.

"I agree," Nick said, interrupting her pleasant descent into numbness. "It is too much of a coincidence. But I can't just haul Ray Howard in for questioning, can I?"

Her eyes flew open, and she sat up. "Not Howard. Father Keller."

"Are you nuts? I can't haul in a priest. You really can't believe a Catholic priest could kill little boys."

"He fits the profile. I need to find out more about his background, but, yes, I do believe a priest is capable."

"I don't. It's crazy." He avoided her eyes and gulped his brandy. "The community would hang me by my thumbs if I hauled in a priest for questioning. Especially this Father Keller. He's like Superman with a collar. Jesus, O'Dell, you're way off target."

"Just listen to me for a minute. You said yourself it looked like Danny Alverez didn't put up a fight. Keller was someone he knew and trusted. Father Francis told us it was unlikely for a layperson post-Vatican II (which would be anyone under the age of thirty-five) to know how to administer the last rites, unless that person had had some training."

"Okay, you check him out. But I need something more than a photo and a piece of baseball card before I haul him in for questioning. In the meantime, I want to do some checking on Howard. You have to admit he's a weird character. What kind of guy dresses in a shirt and tie to clean a church?"

"It's not a crime to dress inappropriately for your job. If it were, you would have been arrested long ago."

He shot her a look, but couldn't hide the smile caught at the corner of his mouth.

"Look, it's late. We're both wiped out. How 'bout we try to get some sleep?" he said, then emptied his glass and set it aside on the floor. He stretched his legs under the quilt. He grabbed a remote from an end table, pressed a few buttons and the lights dimmed. She smiled at his handy little toy for his romantic romps in front of the fire. Why did she find herself almost disappointed that she didn't need to worry about this being one of them?

"Maybe I should go back to the hotel."

"Come on, O'Dell. Your clothes are still wet. All your stuff's labeled dry-clean. 1 couldn't just stick them in the dryer. Look, I'm too tired to make a pass, if that's what you're worried about."

"No, it's not that," she said. "I don't usually sleep much. I might just keep you awake."

"What do you mean you don't sleep?" He slumped down next to her, his head almost touching her arm. He closed his eyes, and she noticed how long his eyelashes were.

"I haven't been able to sleep for over a month now. If I do, I usually have nightmares."

"I imagine with the stuff you see, it's hard not to have nightmares. Did something in particular happen?"

"Not anything I care to discuss."

He stared at her as though trying to look deep inside her. Then he sat up.

"Actually, I think I have a remedy for nightmares. It works with Timmy when he sleeps over."

"Well, then, it can't be more brandy."

"No." He smiled. "You hang on to someone else real tight while you fall asleep."

"Nick, I don't think that's a good idea."

His face was serious again. "Maggie, this isn't some cheap trick to get close to you. I just want to help. Will you let me do that?"

When she didn't answer, he slid closer. Slowly, he put his arm around her as though waiting, giving her plenty of opportunity to protest. When she didn't, he put his hand on her shoulder and gently pulled her into him so that her face rested hot against his chest. She heard his heart pound in her ear. Her own heart beat so noisily it was difficult to distinguish between the two.

"Now relax," he said. "Imagine that nothing can get to you without going through me first."

How could she possibly sleep with her entire body alive, alert and on fire everywhere it touched his?

Maggie awoke groggy. She was cold. The fire had gone out. Nick was no longer beside her. She looked around the dark room and saw the back of his head, asleep on the sofa.

A flicker of light outside the window caught her eye. She sat up. There it was again. A dark shadow with a flashlight passed the window. Her heart began to pound. He had followed them from the river.

"Nick," she whispered, but there was no movement. Her mind raced. Where had she left her gun?

"Nick," she tried again. No response.

The shadow disappeared. She crawled to the bottom of the staircase, watching the window. The room was lit only by the ghostly glow of the moon. She had taken off her gun when they first came in, on her way upstairs. She had laid it on a stand near the staircase. The stand was gone, moved, but where?

Then she heard the twist and click of the doorknob. The metal clicked again and held. The door was locked. She grabbed a small lamp with a heavy metal base and ripped off the shade. She crawled back to the sofa, clutching the lamp.

"Nick," she whispered. "Nick, wake up."

She tugged his shoulder, and his body rolled toward her, tumbling onto the floor. Nick's blue eyes stared up at her, cold and vacant. Blood covered his shirtfront. His throat was slashed, the gaping wound still bleeding.

Then she saw the flicker of light again. The shadow was at the window, looking in, watching her, smiling. It was a face she recognized. It was Albert Stucky.

This time she awoke with a violent flailing of arms, beating and thrashing at anything nearby. Nick grabbed her wrists, preventing her from pummeling his chest. Her body shook, wild convulsions beyond her control.

"Maggie, it's okay." His voice was soft and soothing. "Maggie, you're safe."

She stopped suddenly. Her eyes darted around the room. A fire licked at the huge logs Nick had fed it earlier. The room was lit by the fire's warm yellow glow. Outside the window, snow glittered against the glass. There was no flicker of a flashlight. No Albert Stucky.

"Maggie, are you okay?"

She looked into his eyes. Her own were suddenly very tired. "It didn't work," she whispered. "You lied to me."

"I'm sorry. You were sleeping peacefully for a while. Maybe I wasn't holding you tight enough." He smiled.

She relaxed her fists against his chest while his hands continued to caress her arms, moving up over her elbows, up inside the wide sleeves of the robe. They made it all the way to her shoulders before they began their slow descent. Inch by inch, they warmed her. But the chill was deeper, crawling beneath her skin like ice in her veins.

She leaned against him. He radiated heat. Her cheek brushed against his shirt, the warm cotton fibers. It wasn't enough. She lifted herself away, just enough to give her fingers room while she unbuttoned the rest of his shirt. She avoided his eyes, and felt his body stiffen. His own hands stopped. Perhaps his breathing had, also.

She opened the shirt, resisted the urge to run her hands over the bulging muscles, her fingers through the coarse hair. Instead, she leaned her face against him, listening to the thunder of his heart and allowing his heat to warm her. She only hoped he understood.

His arms wrapped around her waist, but he allowed them no exploration, no caresses. He simply held her body close to his, and this time he held her tightly.

Wednesday, October 29

Maggie had offered to go to Michelle Tanner's with Nick, but he insisted on going alone. Instead, he dropped her off at the hotel.

Her clothes still reeked of muddy river and dried blood. The snow—almost six inches and still falling—clung to her pant legs. The ripped sleeves of her jacket and blouse exposed her wounded shoulder. As she entered the hotel the pimple-faced desk clerk looked up, and his expression immediately changed from a "good morning" nod to an "oh, my God" stare.

"Wow, Agent O'Dell, are you okay?"

"I'm fine. Do I have any messages?"

He handed her a half-dozen pink message slips and a small sealed envelope with "SPECIAL AGENT O'DELL" carefully printed in blue ink.

"What's this?"

"I dunno. It came in the mail slot sometime during the night. I found it on the floor with the morning mail."

"Is there someplace here in town I can buy a coat and boots?"

"There's a John Deere implement store about a mile north of town, but they just have men's stuff."

"Would you mind doing me a favor? Would you call the store and ask them to deliver a jacket? I don't care what it looks like, as long as it's warm and a size small."

"What about boots?"

"Yes, see if they have something close to a woman's size six."

"Got it. They probably don't open until eight or nine."

"That's fine. I'll be in my room all morning. Call me when they're here, and I'll take care of the bill."

"Anything else?"

"Do you have room service?"

"No, but I can get you just about anything from Wanda's. They deliver for free, and we can put it on your hotel tab."

"Great. I'd like a real breakfast—scrambled eggs, sausage, toast, orange juice. Oh, and see if they have cappuccino."

"You got it."

She started down the hall, but something made her stop. "Hey, what's your name?"

"Calvin. Calvin Tate."

"Thanks, Calvin."

Back in her room, she flipped through the messages. One was from Director Cunningham at eleven o'clock, no a.m. or p.m., no message. Why hadn't he called her cellular? Damn, she had forgotten. She needed to report it missing and get a replacement.

Three messages were from Darcy McManus at Channel Five. Two were from Dr. Avery, her mother's therapist, both late last night with instructions to call when possible.

She was guessing the sealed envelope was from the persistent Ms. McManus. She ripped it open and pulled out the three-by-five index card. It took only one glance at the boxy lettering, and her heart began racing. She grabbed the countertop to steady herself, gave up and slid to the floor. Not again. It couldn't happen again. She wouldn't allow it. She hugged her knees to her chest, trying to silence the panic rising inside her.

Then she read the card again:

"WILL YOUR MOTHER BE NEEDING HER LAST RITES SOON?"

It was too early for any traffic, so Nick let the Jeep slide and cut through the drifts on its own. He dreaded telling Michelle Tanner about her son. He wanted those images—no, he *needed* those images of Matthew and Danny out of his mind or he'd be of no use to Mrs. Tanner. So he kept his mind on Maggie. He had never felt so pleasantly uncomfortable in all his many experiences with women. She had managed to turn him inside out. Something he hadn't thought was possible for any one woman to do.

He pulled into the Tanner driveway, almost sliding into the back of a van. It wasn't until he was at the front door that he noticed the KRAP News Radio sign. Panic chewed at his insides. It was awfully early for a simple "how are things going?" interview. He knocked on the screen door. When no one came, he opened it and pounded on the inside door.

Almost immediately it opened. A small, gray-haired woman motioned for him to come into the living room. Then she scurried back into the room and took her seat beside Michelle Tanner on the sofa. A tall, balding man with a tape recorder sat across from them. In the doorway to the kitchen towered a barrel-chested man with a crew cut and thick forearms. He looked familiar, and Nick realized he must be the ex-husband, Matthew's father. A row of candles burned on the fireplace mantel next to a large photo of Matthew and a small crucifix.

"Is it true?" Michelle Tanner looked up at Nick with red, puffy eyes. "Did you find a body last night?"

He reached up and loosened his tie.

"Where did you hear that?"

"Does it fucking matter?" Matthew's father wanted to know.

"Douglas, please," the old woman reprimanded him. "Mr. Melzer here, from the radio, said it was in the *Omaha Journal* this morning."

Melzer held up the paper. SECOND BODY FOUND was emblazoned across the front. Nick didn't need to see the byline. Christine had done it to him again.

"Yes, it's true. I'm sorry I didn't get here sooner."

"You're always just a few steps behind, aren't you, Sheriff?"

"Douglas!" the old woman repeated.

"Is it him?" Michelle looked up at Nick, pleading, hoping.

"Yes. It's Matthew."

He expected the wail and yet wasn't prepared for it. Michelle fell into the old woman's arms, and they rocked back and forth. Douglas Tanner stared at him, leaning against the wall, his anger red on his face.

Then suddenly, in three steps, the man came at him. Nick didn't see the left hook until it slammed into his jaw, knocking him backward into a bookcase. Before he regained his balance, Douglas Tanner came at him again, pounding a fist into his stomach. Nick gasped for breath and stumbled, slipping to his knees. He shook his head and had started to crawl back to his feet when he caught a glimpse of the shiny metal. In one quick burst, Tanner came at him again. Nick jumped out of the way, grabbing for his gun and ripping it from its holster. Tanner froze, a hunting knife gripped expertly in his left hand.

The old woman got up from the sofa and quietly walked over to him. She pulled the knife out of his fist. Then she slapped him across the face.

"Damn it, Mom. What the fuck?"

"I'm sick and tired of you beating on people. Now, apologize to Sheriff Morrelli, Douglas."

"No fucking way. If he had done his job maybe Matthew would still be alive."

"He doesn't need to apologize," Nick said. "Mrs. Tanner, I'm very sorry for your loss. And I apologize for waiting until this morning to tell you. I really didn't mean any disrespect. I just thought it would be better to tell you when you were surrounded by family and friends, rather than pounding on your door in the middle of the night. I promise you, we'll find the man who did this to Matthew."

"Maybe you will, Sheriff," said Douglas Tanner. "But how many more boys will he murder before you do?"

No one had to tell him. Timmy just knew. Matthew was dead, just like Danny Alverez. That was why Uncle Nick and Agent O'Dell left all of a sudden last night. Why his mom sent him to bed early. Why she stayed up almost all night writing for the newspaper on her new laptop computer.

He climbed out of bed early to listen to the school closings on the radio. There had to be at least a half-foot of snow, and it was still coming down. It would be excellent tubing snow, though his mom forbade him to use anything but his boring plastic sled. It was bright orange and stuck out like some kind of emergency vehicle in the snow.

He found her asleep on the sofa, curled up in a tight ball and tangled in Grandma Morrelli's afghan. She looked totally wiped, and he tiptoed into the kitchen, leaving her to sleep.

He tuned the radio to the news station. The announcer was already in the middle of the school announcements.

He was surprised to find an unopened box of Cap'n Crunch between the Cheerios and the Grape-Nuts. Either it had been on sale, or his mom hadn't realized what she had bought. She never let him have the good stuff. As he poured the radio announcer said, "Platte City Elementary and High School will be closed today."

"Yes!" he whispered. And since tomorrow and Friday were a teachers' convention that meant they had five days off. Wow, five whole days! Then he remembered the camping trip, and his excitement was short-lived. Would Father Keller call off the trip because of the snow? He hoped not.

"Timmy?" Wrapped in Grandma's afghan, his mom padded into the kitchen. She looked funny with her hair all tangled and sleep crusted in the corners of her eyes. "Did they close school?"

"Yeah. Five days off. Do you think we'll still go camping?"

She filled the coffee machine, shuffling back and forth.

"I don't know, Timmy. It's only October. Tomorrow it could be forty degrees and the snow will all be gone."

"Is it okay if I go sledding today with some of the guys?"

"You have to dress warm, and you can only use your sled. No inner tubes."

The breakfast Maggie had ordered from Wanda's sat untouched on the small table. She had lost her appetite. It had deserted her while she fought to gain control over her panic. The only thing she touched was the frothy cappuccino. One sip, and she thanked Wanda for having the good sense to invest in a cappuccino maker.

How could one simple note provoke such terror? She had received notes from killers before. They were harmless. It was only a part of the sick game. It came with the territory. If she were going to dig into a killer's psyche, she had to be prepared for the killer to dig back.

Albert Stucky's notes had not been harmless. God, she needed to get past Stucky. He was behind bars and would be there until they executed him. She was safe. At least this note hadn't been accompanied by a severed finger or nipple. Besides, the note was now carefully packaged and on its way Express Mail to a lab at Quantico. Maybe the idiot had sent her his own arrest warrant by leaving his fingerprints or his saliva on the envelope's seal.

By this evening, she would be on a plane home, and this bastard wouldn't be able to play his sick little game. She had done her job, more than what was asked. So why did it feel as if she was running away? Because that was exactly what she was doing. She needed to leave Platte City, Nebraska, before this killer unraveled any more of her already frazzled psyche.

Yes, she needed to leave, and she needed to do it quickly—today—while she still felt in control. She would tie up a few loose ends and then get the hell out. She decided to make a quick phone call. After several rings, a deep male voice answered, "St Margaret's rectory."

"Father Francis, please."

"May I tell him who's calling?"

She couldn't tell whether or not the voice belonged to Howard.

"This is Special Agent Maggie O'Dell. Is this Mr. Howard?"

Instead of answering her question, he said, "One moment, please."

It took several moments. Then… "Maggie O'Dell, what a pleasure to talk with you again."

"Father Francis, I wonder if I might ask you a few more questions."

"Why, certainly." There was a faint click-click.

"Father Francis?"

"I'm still here."

And so was someone else. She'd ask the questions, anyway. Make the intruder sweat.

"What can you tell me about the church's summer camp?"

"Summer camp? That's really Father Keller's project. You might speak to him about it."

"Yes, of course I will. Did he start the project, or was it something St Margaret's has been doing for years?"

"Father Keller started it when he first came. I believe it was an instant success. Of course he had a track record. He had been running one at his previous parish."

"Really? Where was that?"

"Up in Maine. Let's see, I usually have a very good memory. Wood something. Wood River. Yes, Wood River, Maine."

"Thanks for your help, Father."

"Agent O'Dell, is that all you needed to ask me?"

"Yes, but you've been very helpful."

"Actually, I was wondering if you found the answers to your other questions. Your inquiries about Ronald Jeffreys?"

She hesitated. She didn't want to sound abrupt, but she didn't want to discuss what she knew with someone listening.

"Yes, I think we did find the answers. Thanks again for your help."

"Agent O'Dell, I may have some additional information, though I'm not certain of its importance."

"Father Francis, I can't talk right now. I'm expecting an important phone call," she said before he revealed anything more. "Could I meet you perhaps later?"

"Yes, that would be nice. I have morning confessions and then rounds at the hospital this afternoon, so I won't be free until after four o'clock."

"Why don't I meet you in the hospital cafeteria about four-fifteen?"

"I look forward to it. Goodbye, Maggie O'Dell."

She waited for him to hang up, then heard the second set of clicks. There was no mistake. Someone had been listening.

Nick stormed into the sheriff's department, slamming the door so hard the glass rattled. Everyone came to a halt in mid-sentence and mid-stride. They stared at him as though he had gone mad. He felt as if perhaps he had.

"Listen up, everybody. If we have another breach of confidence from this department, I personally will kick the ass of whoever is responsible and see to it that that person never works in law enforcement again."

"Lloyd, I want you to get some men together and check every abandoned shack within a ten-mile radius of Old Church Road. He's keeping these boys somewhere. Maybe it's not here in town. Hal, find out everything you can about a Ray Howard. He's a janitor at the church. Eddie, get over to Sophie Krichek's."

"Nick, you can't be serious. The lady's loony."

"I'm dead serious."

Eddie shrugged, and there was a smirk under the pencil-thin mustache that Nick wanted to knock off.

"Do it this morning, Eddie, and treat it like your job depends on getting the details right." He paused. "Adam, call George Tillie and tell him Agent O'Dell will be assisting him this afternoon with Matthew's autopsy. Then call FBI Agent Weston and get the evidence his forensic team found. I want photos and reports on my desk by one this afternoon.

"Lucy, find out anything you can about a summer church camp

that St Margaret's sponsors. Get together with Max and see if you can connect Aaron Harper and Eric Paltrow to that camp."

He dismissed the group. Lloyd caught up with him down the hall at his office door.

"About checking old shacks. Nick, there's not much out there that we didn't check the first time. There's an old barn about ready to fall down on Woodson's property. Other than a deserted lean-to or grain bin, there isn't anything else. Except for the old church, but it's boarded up tighter than a virgin on Sunday."

"Check the church again, Lloyd. Look for broken windows, footprints, any sign of entry in the last several days."

"Hell, we're not gonna find any footprints with this snow coming down."

"Just check, Lloyd."

Father Francis gathered the newspaper clippings and slid them into his leather portfolio. It had only been three months since Ronald Jeffreys' execution. Three months since he had listened to the confession of the real killer of the Harper and Paltrow boys. He could no longer keep silent. He could no longer preserve the sanctity of a killer's confession. Maybe it wouldn't make a difference, but he had convinced himself that it was the right thing to do.

He shuffled down the hall to the church. His footsteps were the only sound. No one waited for confession. It would be a quiet morning. Still, he entered the small confessional.

Despite his having seen no one in the church, the door in the black cubicle next to him opened within minutes. Father Francis sat up and laid his elbow on the shelf, allowing himself to lean closer to the wire-mesh window between the two small rooms.

"Bless me, Father, for I have killed again."

Oh, dear God. The panic came crashing against the old priest's chest. It was difficult to breathe. Father Francis strained to see beyond the thick wire mesh that separated them. All he could see, though, was a huddled black shadow.

"I killed Danny Alverez and Matthew Tanner. For these sins, I am truly sorry and ask forgiveness."

The voice was disguised, barely audible, as if forced through a mask. Was there anything, anything at all, that he could recognize?

"What is my penance?"

"How can I absolve you of your sins…heinous, horrible sins…if you only intend to do them again?"

"No, y-you don't understand. I only bring them peace," the voice sputtered. He obviously hadn't come prepared for a confrontation, Father Francis realized with some degree of satisfaction. He had come only for absolution and to do his penance.

"I cannot absolve you of your sins if you simply intend to go out and do it again." Father Francis' strong, unflinching voice surprised him.

"You must…you have to."

"I absolved you once before, and you've made a mockery of the sacrament by committing the sin again, not once, but twice."

"I am truly sorry for my sins and ask forgiveness from God," he tried again, mechanically saying the phrase like a child memorizing it for the first time.

"You must prove your remorse," Father Francis said, suddenly feeling powerful. Perhaps he could influence this black shadow, make him face his demons, stop him once and for all. "You must show your repentance."

"Yes. Yes, I will. Just tell me what my penance is."

"Go prove your repentance and come back in a month."

There was a pause.

"You aren't absolving me?"

"If you can prove your worthiness by not killing, I will consider absolving you then."

"You will not give me absolution?"

"Come back in a month."

There was silence, but the shadow made no motion to leave. Father Francis leaned closer to the wire mesh, again straining to see into the pitch-black cube. There was a soft smack, then a hiss as a spray of saliva flew through the wire mesh, hitting him in the face.

"I'll see you in hell, Father." The low guttural tone sent shivers down Father Francis' spine. And though the saliva dripped down his chin, he couldn't move even to wipe at it. When he heard the door open and the shadow exit, his paralyzed body made no attempt to follow or look out after him.

No one else came in. Perhaps the snow had kept other sinners at home, he thought absently. Which meant no one had seen the shadowy figure enter or exit the confessional.

Finally, he fumbled for a handkerchief and wiped his face. He eased himself out of the hard chair and peered out. The church was empty and silent.

On the way to his office he noticed that someone had left the door to the wine cellar open. He stopped in the doorway and peered down the dark steps. A draft made him shiver. Was there a shadow? Down in the far corner, was someone huddled in the darkness?

He stepped onto the first step, clinging to the railing. Was it his imagination, or was someone huddled between the stacked wine crates and the concrete wall?

He never saw the figure behind him. He only felt the violent shove that sent him sailing down the steps headfirst. His frail body crashed against the wall, and he tumbled the rest of the way. He was still conscious when he heard the steps creak, one by one by one. The sound of the slow descent sent terror through his aching body. He opened his mouth to scream but only a moan erupted. He couldn't move, couldn't run. His right leg was on fire and twisted beneath him.

The last step creaked just above him. He lifted his head in time to see a blaze of white canvas smash into his face. Then darkness.

Christine treated herself to Wanda's homemade chicken noodle soup and buttercrust rolls. Corby had given her the morning off, but she had brought her notepad and jotted down ideas for tomorrow's article.

Timmy had called and asked whether he and his friends could have lunch at the rectory with Father Keller. The priest had joined them sledding on Cutty's Hill and, to make up for the inevitably canceled camping trip, he had invited the boys for roasted hot dogs and marshmallows by the fireplace in the rectory.

"Great series of articles, Christine," Angie Clark said as she refilled Christine's cup with more coffee.

Caught off guard, Christine swallowed the bite of warm bread. "Thanks." She smiled and wiped a napkin across her mouth. "Your mom's rolls are still the best around."

She watched Angie greet two burly construction workers who came in and began peeling off their layers of jackets, hats and overalls. She sipped the steaming coffee and jotted down "coroner's report". George Tillie was an old family friend. He and her dad had been hunting buddies for years. Maybe George could supply her with some new information.

Suddenly, the volume on the corner television blasted the room. She looked up just as Wanda Clark waved at her.

"Christine, listen to this."

The news anchor on CNN had just mentioned Platte City, Nebraska. A graphic behind him showed its location while he talked about the bizarre series of murders. They flashed Christine's Sunday headline, FROM THE GRAVE, SERIAL KILLER STILL GRIPS COMMUNITY WITH BOY'S RECENT MURDER and described the murders and Jeffreys' killing spree six years before.

"A source close to the investigation says the sheriff's department still has no clues, and that the only suspect on their list is one who was executed three months ago."

Christine cringed at the hint of sarcasm, and for the first time she sympathized with Nick. The volume went down, and she went back to her notes.

Her concentration was broken when Eddie Gillick slid into the booth next to her, shoving her up against the window. "What do you think you're doing?" she demanded.

"It was bad enough when you tricked me into giving you a quote for your newspaper article, but now your little brother is giving me chicken-shit assignments, so I figure you also told him I was your anonymous source."

"Look, Deputy Gillick—"

"No, hey, it's Eddie, remember?"

"I didn't exactly tell Nick. He—"

"No, that's okay, because the way I figure it, now you owe me one."

She felt his hand on her knee, and the look of contempt in his eyes immobilized her. His hand moved up her thigh and under her skirt before she wrestled it away. The corner of his mustache twitched into a smile as she felt the color rise into her face.

He slid out of the booth, ran a hand over his slicked-down black hair and replaced his hat. Then he sauntered back down the aisle and out into the street.

The door flung open just in time for Nick to see Maggie race back across her hotel room.

"Come on in!" she yelled as she poked at the keyboard of her laptop computer. Then she stood back and watched the screen. "I'm accessing some information from Quantico's database. It's proving to be very interesting."

She glanced up at him, then did a double take. "What happened to your face?"

"Christine didn't wait. There was an article in this morning's paper."

"And Michelle Tanner saw it before you got there?"

"Someone told her about it."

"She hit you?"

"No. Her ex-husband, Matthew's dad, sort of let me have it."

"Jesus, Morrelli, don't you know how to duck?"

The anger must have still been in his eyes, because she quickly added, "Sorry. You should put some ice on it."

She went back to the computer.

"Here it is," she said, watching the screen fill with what looked like newspaper articles.

He leaned forward. "The *Wood River Gazette*, November 1989. Where is Wood River?"

"Maine." She poked at the scroll button, scanning the headlines. Then she stopped and pointed to one.

"BOY'S MUTILATED BODY FOUND NEAR RIVER. This sounds

familiar," he said. He started reading the article that stretched over three columns of the front page.

"Guess who was a junior pastor at Wood River's St Mary's Catholic Church?"

He stopped, looked back at her and rubbed his jaw. "You still don't have any evidence. It's all circumstantial. Why didn't this case come up during Jeffreys' trial?"

"There was no need. From what I've been able to find out, a transient working at St Mary's Church took the blame."

"Maybe he did it. How did you find out about it?"

"Just a hunch. When I talked to Father Francis this morning, he told me Father Keller had started a similar summer camp at his previous parish in Wood River, Maine."

"So you looked for murdered boys in the area at the time he was there."

"I didn't have to look very hard. This murder matches right down to the X. Circumstantial or not, Father Keller needs to be considered a suspect." She closed down the program and shut off the computer.

"I've got to meet your coroner George Tillie in about an hour," she said, "then I'm meeting with Father Francis." She started taking clothes out of the closet and laying them on the bed. "I need to leave for Richmond tonight. My mother's in the hospital." She avoided looking at him while she pulled more of her things from drawers.

"Jesus, Maggie, is she okay?"

"Sort of…I guess she will be. I'll have some information for you on disk. Can you access Microsoft Word?"

"Sure…yeah, I think so." Her matter-of-fact attitude flustered him. Was something wrong, or was she simply concerned about her mother?

"You're not coming back, are you?" The realization struck him like another fist to the jaw. It also stopped her. She turned to face him, though her eyes darted from his to the blank computer screen, to his, to the mess on the bed. She had never had a tough time meeting his eyes before.

"Technically, I finished what I was asked to do. You have a profile and maybe even a suspect. I'm not even sure that I need to be involved with this second autopsy."

"So that's it?"

"I'm sure the Bureau will send someone else to help you."

"I'm gonna miss you." The words surprised him. He hadn't meant to say them out loud.

She stopped, straightened and turned slowly, this time meeting his eyes. Those luscious brown eyes made him weak at the knees, like a high-school kid admitting to his first girlfriend that he liked her. Jesus, what was wrong with him?

"You've been a pain in the ass, O'Dell, but I'm going to miss you giving me a hard time." There. He corrected his slip.

She smiled.

"Do you need a lift to the airport?"

"No, I have a rental I have to turn in."

"Well, have a good flight." It sounded pathetic. What he really wanted to do was wrap his arms around her and convince her to stay. He crossed the room to leave in three long strides.

"Nick."

He stopped at the door, his hand on the handle. She paused, and in a brief moment he saw her change her mind about whatever she was going to say.

"Good luck," she said.

He nodded and left, feeling lead in his shoes and an ache in his chest.

Maggie watched the door close as her hands strangled and twisted a silk blouse.

Why didn't she just tell Nick about the note, about Albert Stucky? He had understood about the nightmares. Maybe he'd understand about this. Maybe he'd understand that she just couldn't allow herself to be psychologically poked and probed by another madman. Not now. Not when she felt so vulnerable, so damn fragile.

The phone rang, and she jumped as if it were a gunshot. She had already talked to Dr. Avery. Her mother had survived the seventy-two-hour suicide watch and was doing better.

She grabbed the phone. "Special Agent O'Dell."

"Maggie, why are you still there? I thought you were coming home."

"Hi, Greg. I'm catching a flight tonight."

"Good, so that dunce actually gave you my message last night?"

"What dunce?"

"The one I talked to last night who picked up your cellular. He said you must have dropped it and couldn't come to the phone."

Her grip tightened. Her pulse raced. "What time was that?"

"About midnight here. Why?"

"What did you tell him?"

"Oh, for cryin' out loud. That asshole didn't give you the message, did he?"

"Greg." She tried to stay calm, to keep the scream from clawing its way out of her throat. "I lost my cellular phone last night when I was chasing the killer. There's a good chance he was the one you talked to."

"How was I supposed to know?"

"I'm not blaming you, Greg. Just, please, try to remember what you told him."

"Nothing really…just to call me and that your mother wasn't doing too well."

She leaned back on the bed, sinking her head into the pillows and closing her eyes.

"Maggie, when you get home we need to talk."

Yes, they would talk on a beach somewhere, sipping fruity drinks, the ones with little umbrellas stuffed in them.

"I want you to quit the Bureau," he said, and then she knew there would never be a sunny beach for them.

He heard the sledders squealing and giggling. He lay there, pressed into the snow, concealed by snow-laced prairie grass. They should have gone home while the throbbing in his head was silent. Why hadn't they gone home? It would be getting dark soon. Would there be plates set on a dinner table waiting for them or only a note and a microwave dinner? Would their parents be there to make sure they took off their wet clothing? Would anyone be there to tuck them into bed?

He couldn't stop the memories, and he no longer tried. He could see himself at twelve, wearing a green army jacket with little lining to keep out the cold. His patched jeans allowed drafts to assault his body. He hadn't owned a pair of boots. The snowfall had been over ten inches and the entire town ground to a stop, leaving his stepfather with nowhere to go except his mother's bedroom. He had been told to leave the house, to "go play in the snow with his friends". Only he had no friends.

After hours of sitting in the cold backyard, he had gone back to the house only to find the door locked. Through the thin wood and fragile glass, he had listened to his mother's screams and moans—pain and pleasure indistinguishable. Did sex have to hurt? He couldn't imagine growing to enjoy such pain. And he remembered feeling ashamed because he had been relieved. He knew as long as his stepfather slammed into his mother, he wouldn't slam into him.

It was while he sat in the bitter white cold that day that he had plotted, a plot so simple it required only a ball of string. The next morning when his stepfather retreated to his basement workshop, he would come back up on a stretcher. How could he have known that his mother would go down to the basement first that morning? That morning when his life had ended; when that horrible wicked little boy had ended his mother's life!

Suddenly, he felt someone above him, breathing and sniffing. He slowly looked up to find a black dog within inches of his face. The dog bared its teeth, emitting a low growl. Without warning, his hands shot out at the dog's throat and the growl became a quiet whine, a stifled gurgle, then silence.

He watched the boys dressed in thick parkas running and jumping with stiff legs and arms. Finally, they gathered up their sledding contraptions and said their goodbyes. One boy called for the dog several times but gave up easily to catch up with his friends. They separated and headed in different directions, three one way, two another, while one crossed the church's parking lot alone.

The sky changed from light gray to slate. Streetlights blinked on one at a time. There wasn't a single vehicle or pedestrian in sight when he climbed into his car. He pulled the ski mask back on. On the seat next to him, he laid out a fresh handkerchief, meticulously as though it were already a part of the ceremony. He brought a vial out of his coat pocket, cracked it and anointed the white linen. Then he kept the headlights off and the engine soft as he slowly followed the boy who dragged his bright orange plastic sled behind him.

Nick couldn't help wondering whether a real sheriff could have saved Matthew Tanner. But Platte City had a skirt chasing college quarterback with a law degree, absolutely no experience and only his father's name and reputation to win him the right to call himself sheriff and to carry a badge and a gun. Now that Maggie was leaving, it was up to him to take control. He just wished he knew how the hell to do that.

He entered the courthouse and immediately wanted to flee in the other direction. The huge marble lobby echoed with the chatter of reporters. Cords and cables snaked over the floor. Bright lights blinded him and a dozen microphones were shoved into his face.

Darcy McManus, an ex-beauty queen turned TV anchor, barricaded the staircase with her tall, lean body.

"Sheriff, do you have any suspects yet?"

"I have no comment to make at this time."

"Is it true Matthew Tanner's body was decapitated?" a man in an expensive double-breasted suit wanted to know.

"Jesus. Where the hell did you hear that?"

"Then it's true?"

"No. Absolutely not."

"Sheriff, what about the rumor that you've ordered the exhumation of Ronald Jeffreys' grave? Do you believe Jeffreys wasn't the one executed?"

"Was the boy sexually assaulted?"

"Sheriff Morrelli, are we dealing with a serial killer?"

"Will your father be heading the investigation now?" the man in the double-breasted suit asked.

"Have you tracked down the blue pickup?"

Nick spun around, almost losing his balance. "What's that about my father? Why in the world would my father head this investigation?"

"He *did* catch Ronald Jeffreys," Darcy McManus said into her channel's camera, and only then did Nick realize they had been filming this whole fiasco. He avoided looking into the camera and stared at the man in the suit.

"When your father talked to us earlier, he made it sound—"

"He's here?" Nick exclaimed.

"Yes, and he made it sound as though he had returned to help with the investigation. I believe his exact words were…" the man flipped through his notes "…'I've done this before. I know what to look for. You can bet this guy's not getting by this old bloodhound.' I'm not familiar with bloodhounds, but I did interpret it to mean he was here in a professional capacity."

Nick turned and ran up the staircase. He crashed through the sheriff's department doors, smacking the glass against a metal trash can and a wall. A spider crack raced across the bottom of one of the doors, but no one seemed to notice. Instead, all eyes stared at Nick, their attention diverted from the tall gray-haired man in the center of them.

The same group Nick couldn't get to check a lead without a groan or a question was gathered around this distinguished-looking gentleman, an aging prophet with the beginning of a paunch and a pair of bushy eyebrows that were now raised in indignation.

"Slow down, son. You just damaged government property," Antonio Morrelli said, pointing to the crack in the glass.

Maggie sipped her Scotch and watched from a corner table as she tried to determine which of the airport-lounge customers were business travelers and which were vacationers. The storm had delayed flights, hers included, and had packed the small, poorly lit lounge. Her green and black John Deere jacket was stretched across the chair opposite her to prevent any unwanted company. She had already checked her luggage, everything except her laptop computer, which was secure underneath the John Deere green. She thought about calling St Margaret's again. She was beginning to think something dreadful may have happened. Otherwise, why would Father Francis have stood her up at the hospital? And why was there no one at the church rectory to answer the phone?

She wanted to call Nick, had in fact dialed the number but then hung up. He had enough things to handle without checking on her hunches. Besides, she was running out of change for the pay phone and had spent her last ten-dollar bill on this and the two previous Scotches. Not much of a dinner, but after spending the afternoon slicing Matthew Tanner's small body, weighing pieces of him and poking through his tiny organs, she had decided she deserved a dinner of Scotch.

The marks on Matthew's inside thigh had indeed been human bite marks. Poor George Tillie had tried to come up with several other theories before giving in to the realization that the killer had bitten Matthew over and over again in the same spot, making it impossible to register a set of dental prints. What made matters worse and more bizarre—the bites had occurred hours after Matthew was dead.

The killer didn't return to the scene of the crime only to watch the police. He continued his absurd fascination with the victim's body. He was slipping from his carefully planned ritual.

Maggie had told George they should look for smudges of semen; that the killer may have masturbated this time, while biting the dead boy, and may have smeared some on the victim. The old coroner's face had turned scarlet as he mumbled something about doing his job in private.

"Excuse me, ma'am." The young bartender stood over her table. "The gentleman at the end of the bar bought you another Scotch." He set the glass in front of her. "And he asked me to give you this."

Maggie recognized the envelope and the boxy handwriting before he handed it to her. Her stomach lurched, her pulse quickened. She stood up.

"Which man?" She stretched to see over the crowd. The bartender did the same, then shrugged his shoulders. "He must have left."

"What did he look like?"

"Tall, dark hair, maybe twenty-eight, maybe thirty. Look, I didn't pay a whole lot of attention. Is there a problem with…?"

She shoved past him and pushed through the crowd, racing out into the bright airport walkway. It stretched straight in both directions. There was a family with three children, several businessmen carrying laptops and briefcases, an airport employee pushing a handcart, two gray-haired women. But there was no tall, dark-haired man without luggage.

She ran toward the escalator at the far end. The escalator went up and down. She chose up and leant over the handrail to see down. Again, the array of passengers didn't include a tall, dark-haired man. He was gone. He had slipped by her again.

She made her way back to the lounge. No one had attempted to take over her table. Even the envelope leaned against the fresh drink where the bartender had left it.

She took the envelope carefully by a corner. The seal broke easily, and she slipped the index card out onto the table without touching it. In the same boxy lettering, the note said:

SORRY TO SEE YOU LEAVE SO SOON. PERHAPS I CAN STOP BY YOUR CONDO THE NEXT TIME I'M IN THE CREST RIDGE AREA. SAY HI TO GREG FOR ME.

From down on the sidewalk, he had seen Maggie O'Dell inside, scrambling up the escalator. He had to admit she moved quite nicely—definitely a runner. He imagined those strong, athletic legs looked good in a pair of tight shorts, though the image didn't much interest him.

He pushed the handcart aside and removed the cap and jacket he had borrowed from the sleeping airport employee. He rolled them into a ball and shoved them into a trash can.

He had left the Lexus with the radio blaring in the loading zone. With the radio and the jets overhead, no one would ever hear Timmy, should he wake up sooner than expected. Besides, the trunk was tight, almost soundproof.

He got into the car just as a security guard with a pad of tickets started in his direction. He squealed away from the curb and zipped around the unloading vehicles. It would be pitch-black by the time he got Timmy settled in, but seeing the look on Special Agent O'Dell's face had made the detour worthwhile.

The wind had picked up, creating swirls of snow and promising drifts by morning. The kerosene heater, lantern and sleeping bag in the backseat, originally packed for the camping trip, would come in handy, after all. Perhaps he would drive through McDonald's on the way. Timmy loved Big Macs, and he found himself getting hungry.

He was in control again.

49

"This guy's making a fuckin' spectacle out of you," Antonio Morrelli lectured Nick while looking quite comfortable behind Nick's desk, twirling back and forth in the leather chair that was once his.

"You need to spend some time with those TV people," his father continued. "Reassure them you know what you're doing. Last night that journalist made you sound like some country hick who couldn't find his own ass with a flashlight. Goddamn it, Nick!"

"Did Mom come with you?" Nick asked from his window perch without looking at his father, ignoring his insults.

"She stayed with your aunt Minnie and the RV down in Houston," his father answered, but his look told Nick he wouldn't be sidetracked from the real subject. "You need to start hauling in suspects off the street. You know, the usual scumbags. Bring 'em in for questioning. Make it look like you're on top of things."

"I do have a couple of suspects," Nick said.

"Great, let's haul them in. Judge Murphy could probably get a search warrant by morning. Who are your suspects?"

"One of them is Father Michael Keller."

The older man shook his head and frustration creased the leather-like forehead.

"What the fuck are you trying to pull, Nick? A fucking priest—the media will crucify you. Is this your idea, or that pretty little FBI agent the guys told me about?"

"Father Keller fits Agent O'Dell's profile."

"I'm sure O'Dell makes a good omelette for breakfast after a night of fucking. Doesn't mean you should listen to her."

"This is my investigation, my decision, and I'm bringing in Father Keller for questioning."

"Fine." His father held up his hands in surrender. "Make a fucking asshole of yourself."

The house was dark when Christine pulled into the driveway. She loaded the warm pizza box on top of her laptop computer and realized she'd probably be eating the pizza by herself if Timmy was still at one of his friends' houses. Snow was falling heavily as she kicked the front door closed and made her way to the kitchen, stopping by the answering machine. No blinking red light, no messages. How many times did she have to tell Timmy to call and leave a message?

She threw her coat over a kitchen chair and piled her computer and handbag onto its seat. The pizza's aroma reminded her how hungry she was. After Eddie Gillick's visit at Wanda's, she had lost her appetite and left most of her lunch unfinished.

She poured herself a glass of wine, tucked a folded newspaper under her arm and scooped up a piece of pizza, using only a napkin as a plate. Hands filled, she kicked off her shoes and padded into the living room, finding refuge on the soft sofa. No food was allowed in the living room, especially on the sofa. She expected Timmy to come in at any moment and catch her in the act.

She set her dinner on the glass coffee table and unfolded the newspaper. This evening's paper carried the same headline from the morning: SECOND BODY FOUND. Underneath, she had now confirmed that the body was Matthew Tanner's. Tonight's article also included a quote from George Tillie. She found the paragraph and reread her handiwork, letting George confirm that the murders were the work of a serial killer, since Nick wouldn't.

She finished her wine. Another piece of pizza sounded good, but suddenly she was too exhausted to move. In minutes, she was fast asleep.

"Why don't you eat some of your Big Mac?" the man in the dead president's mask was saying.

Timmy curled into the corner. The bedsprings squeaked each time he moved. His eyes darted around the small room lit only by a lantern on an old crate. The light created its own creepy shadows on the walls with spiderweb cracks. He was shaking, and he couldn't control it. He was shaking because he was scared, because he didn't know where he was or how he had gotten here.

The tall man in the mask had been nice so far. When he had stopped Timmy by the church to ask for directions, he had been wearing a black ski mask, the kind robbers wore in the movies. But it was cold out, and the man had seemed lost and confused but not scary. Even when the man had gotten out of his car to show Timmy a map, Timmy hadn't felt scared. There was something familiar about him. That was when the man had grabbed him and shoved a white cloth against his face. Timmy couldn't remember anything else, except waking up here.

The wind howled through the rotted boards that covered the windows, but the room was warm. Timmy noticed a kerosene heater in the corner.

"You really should eat. I know you haven't had anything since lunch."

Timmy stared at the man, who looked more ridiculous than scary dressed in a sweater, jeans and bright white Nikes that looked new except that one shoestring was knotted together. A pair of huge, black, dripping rubber boots sat by the door on a paper sack.

It struck Timmy as odd that such new Nikes could already have a broken and knotted shoestring.

He tried to think of the president's name—the one the mask resembled. It was the guy with the big nose who had to resign. Why couldn't he think of his name? They had memorized the presidents just last year.

"Are you cold? Is there anything else I can get you?" the man asked, and Timmy shook his head. "Tomorrow I'll bring you some baseball cards and comic books." The man got up, took the lantern from the crate and started to leave.

"Can I keep the lantern?"

The man looked back at him, and Timmy could see the eyes through the mask's eyeholes. In the light of the lantern, they were sparkling as if the man were smiling.

"Sure, Timmy. I'll leave the lantern."

Timmy didn't remember telling the man his name. Did he know him?

The man set the lantern back down on the crate, pulled on his thick rubber boots and left, locking the door with several clicks and clacks from the outside. Timmy waited, listening over the thumping of his heart. He counted out two minutes, and when he was sure the man wouldn't return, he looked around the room again. The rotted slats over the window were his best bet.

He crawled off the bed and tripped over his sled on the floor. He started for the window when something caught his leg. He looked down to find a silver handcuff around his ankle with a thick metal chain padlocked to the bedpost. He yanked at the chain, but even the metal-framed bed wouldn't budge. He dropped to his knees and tore at the handcuff, pulling and tugging until his fingers were red and his ankle sore. Suddenly, he stopped struggling.

He looked around the room again, and then he knew. This was where Danny and Matthew had been taken.

"Oh, God," he prayed out loud, the tremble in his voice scaring him even more. "Please don't let me get dead like Danny and Matthew."

Then he tried to think of something—anything—else, and he began naming the presidents out loud, starting with, "Washington, Adams, Jefferson…"

After making several phone calls and getting no response, Nick decided to drive over to the rectory. He couldn't go home. Eventually, that would be where his father would go. That was the one disadvantage of living in the family home—the family moved back whenever they wanted.

The rectory was lit up inside and outside as if for a party. Yet Nick waited a long time before anyone answered his knock.

Father Keller opened the door, dressed in a long black robe.

"Sheriff Morrelli, sorry for the delay. I was taking a shower," he said.

"I did try calling first."

"Really? I've been here all evening, except I'm afraid I can't hear the phone from my bathroom. Come in."

A freshly fed fire roared in the huge fireplace that was the living room's center of attraction. A colorful Oriental rug and several easy chairs sat in front.

"Please sit down." Father Keller pointed to one of the chairs. "Can I get you some coffee?"

"No, thanks. This won't take long." Nick unzipped his jacket and pulled out a notepad and pen.

"I'm afraid there's not much I can tell you, Sheriff. I think he simply had a heart attack."

"Excuse me?"

"Father Francis. That is why you're here, isn't it?"

"What about Father Francis?"

"Oh, dear, I'm sorry. I thought that was why you were here. We think he had a heart attack and fell down the basement steps sometime this morning."

"Is he okay?"

"I'm afraid he's dead, God rest his soul."

"Jesus, I'm sorry. I didn't know."

"I'm sure it's a shock. It certainly was for all of us. You served mass for Father Francis, didn't you? At the old St Margaret's?"

"Seems like ages ago." Nick stared into the fire, remembering how fragile the old priest had looked when he and Maggie questioned him.

"Excuse me, Sheriff, but if you're not here about Father Francis, what is it I can help you with?"

"Actually, I just had a few questions for you about…about the summer church camp you sponsor."

"The church camp?"

Was the look one of confusion or alarm? Nick couldn't be sure.

"Both Danny Alverez and Matthew Tanner were at your church camp this past summer."

"Really?"

"You didn't know?"

"We had over two hundred boys last summer."

"Do you have pictures taken with all of them?"

"Excuse me?"

"My nephew, Timmy Hamilton, has a photo of about fifteen to twenty boys with you and Mr. Howard."

"Oh, yes." Father Keller raked his fingers through his thick hair, and only then did Nick realize it wasn't wet. "The canoe photos. Not all the boys qualified for the races, but, yes, we did take pictures with the ones who qualified. Mr. Howard is a volunteer counselor. I've tried to include Ray in as many church activities as possible ever since he left the seminary last year and came to work for us."

Howard had been in a seminary. Nick waited for more.

"So Timmy Hamilton is your nephew? He's a great kid."

"Yes, yes, he is."

Did he dare ask more questions about Howard or was the distraction exactly what Father Keller wanted?

"You started a similar church camp for boys at your previous parish, didn't you, Father Keller? In Maine. Wood River, I believe it was."

"That's right."

"Why did you leave Wood River?"

"I was offered an associate pastor position here. You might say it was a promotion."

"Were you aware of the murder of a little boy in the Wood River area just before you left?"

"I'm not sure I understand your line of questioning, Sheriff. Are you accusing me of having some knowledge about these murders?"

"I'm just checking as many leads as possible." Suddenly, Nick felt ridiculous. How could Maggie ever have led him to believe that a Catholic priest was capable of murder? Then it hit him. "Father Keller, how did you know I served mass for Father Francis at the old St Margaret's?"

"I'm not sure. Father Francis must have mentioned it to me."

Again the priest avoided Nick's eyes. A sudden knock at the door interrupted them, and Father Keller quickly got up.

"I'm certainly not dressed for company."

He smiled at Nick as he tucked in the lapels of his robe and tightened its cinch.

"Excuse me."

Nick got up and paced the large room. Huge built-in bookcases made up one wall. There were few decorations—a highly polished, dark wooden crucifix with an unusual pointed end. It almost looked like a dagger. There were also several original paintings. The swishes of bright color were hypnotic, swirling yellows and reds in a field of vibrant purple.

Then Nick saw them. Tucked away around the side of the brick fireplace that jutted out into the room was a pair of black rubber boots, still plastered with snow and sitting on an old mat. Had Father Keller lied about not being out this evening? Or perhaps the boots belonged to Ray Howard.

From the foyer Nick heard voices raised. He hurried to the entrance, where he saw Father Keller trying to remain calm and cool while Maggie O'Dell bombarded him with questions.

Maggie's voice was loud, shrill and belligerent—this from a woman who appeared to be the essence of control.

"I want to see Father Francis now," she said and pushed past Father Keller. She almost ran into Nick.

"Nick, what are you doing here?"

"I could ask you the same thing. Don't you have a flight to catch?"

"Flights are delayed. The snow—or hadn't you noticed?"

"Maggie, you haven't met Father Michael Keller. Father Keller, this is Special Agent Maggie O'Dell."

"So you're Keller. What have you done with Father Francis?"

Again, the belligerence. Nick couldn't figure out this new approach.

"I tried to explain…" Father Keller began.

"Yes, you do have some explaining to do. Father Francis was supposed to meet me at the hospital this afternoon. He never showed up." She looked to Nick. "I've been calling here all afternoon and evening."

"Maggie, why don't you come in and calm down?"

"I want some answers. I want to know what the hell's going on here."

"There was an accident this morning," Nick explained. "Father Francis fell down some basement steps. I'm afraid he's dead."

"An accident?" Then she looked up at Father Keller. "Nick, are you sure it was an accident?"

"Maggie…"

"How can you be sure he wasn't pushed? Has anyone examined the body? I'll do the autopsy myself if necessary."

"An autopsy?" Father Keller repeated.

"Maggie, he was old and frail," said Nick.

"Exactly. So why would he be going down basement steps?"

"Actually, it's our wine cellar," Father Keller explained.

Maggie stared at him. "What exactly are you implying?"

"Implying? I'm not implying anything."

"Maggie, maybe we should go," Nick said, taking her gently by the arm. Immediately she wrenched it from his grasp and shot him a look that made him take a step backward. She stared at Father Keller again, then suddenly pushed past both of them and headed for the door.

Nick caught up with her on the sidewalk. He reached for her arm to slow her down, but thought better of it and simply increased his pace to stay alongside her.

"What the hell was that about?" he demanded.

"He's lying. I doubt that it was an accident."

"Father Francis was an old man, Maggie."

"He had something important to tell me. When we talked on the phone this morning, I could tell someone else was listening in. I'm guessing it was Keller. Don't you see, Nick?" She came to a halt and turned to look at him. "Whoever was listening decided to stop Father Francis before he had a chance to tell me whatever was so important. An autopsy may show whether or not he was pushed. I'll do it myself if—"

"Maggie, stop. There's not going to be an autopsy. Keller didn't push anybody, and I don't think he had anything to do with the murders. This is nuts."

Her face went white, her shoulders slumped, and her eyes were watery.

"Maggie?"

She turned and hurried off the sidewalk into the snow, back behind the rectory and out of the bright streetlights. Clinging to a tree, she bent over and began retching. Nick grimaced and kept his distance. Now he understood the belligerence. Maggie O'Dell was drunk.

He waited until she finished, standing guard in the shadows, keeping his back to her in case she was now sober enough to be embarrassed.

"Nick."

When he turned, she was walking away from him, behind the rectory toward a grove of trees that separated the church property from Cutty's Hill.

"Nick, look." She stopped and pointed. Then he saw it. Tucked back in the trees was an old blue pickup with wooden side racks.

"I'll get Judge Murphy to issue a search warrant first thing in the morning," Nick was explaining when they got back to Maggie's hotel room. She was lucky to get it back with there being so many stranded motorists. She wished that he would just shut up. Her head ached. She threw her laptop and jacket onto the bed and lay down next to them.

Nick stood in the doorway. "I couldn't believe the way you were going at Keller. Jesus, I thought you were going to punch him."

"Either come in or leave, but don't stand in the open doorway. I have a reputation, after all."

He pulled a chair to the edge of the bed where she could see him and not have to move.

"So what did you do, decide to have a little going-away party?"

"It seemed like a good idea at the time."

She pulled herself up on one elbow and dug through her jacket pockets. She handed him the small envelope and lay back down.

"I was in the airport lounge when the bartender gave me that—said a guy at the bar asked him to deliver it to me. Only the guy was gone by the time I got it."

She watched him read it. He looked confused, and she remembered she hadn't told him about the first note.

"It's from the killer."

"How does he know where you live and your husband's name?"

"He's probing me, investigating me, digging into my background just like I'm doing to him."

"Jesus, Maggie."

"It comes with the territory. It's not that unusual." She closed her eyes. "No one answered the phone at the rectory for hours. Plenty of time to make a trip to the airport and back."

When she opened her eyes, Nick was studying her. She sat up, suddenly feeling exposed under his concerned gaze.

"Maggie, are you okay?"

She looked into his blue eyes and felt the electrical current even before his fingers touched her face and his palm caressed her cheek. Suddenly, she vaulted from his touch, scrambling from the bed and from him. Her breathing was uneven, and she steadied herself with both hands, leaning against the dresser. She looked up and saw him in the mirror, behind her. Their eyes met in the reflection, and she held his gaze even though what she saw in his eyes made her stomach flutter. This time it wasn't because of the alcohol.

She watched as he came up behind her, so close she felt his breath on her neck even before he leaned down to kiss it. The Packers jersey had slipped off her shoulder, and she watched in the mirror as his soft, wet lips moved slowly, deliberately from her neck to her shoulder to her back. By the time they moved up her neck again, she had trouble breathing.

"Nick, what are you doing?"

"I've wanted to touch you for days."

His tongue flicked at her earlobe, and her knees went weak.

"This isn't a good idea." It came out as a whisper, not the least bit convincing. And it certainly didn't stop his big, steady hands from coming around her waist, one palm flat against her stomach, sending a shiver down her back and the flutter from her stomach down between her legs.

"Nick." It was useless. She couldn't talk, couldn't breathe, and his gentle, urgent mouth was devouring her in soft, wet explorations while his hands made their way up her body.

She watched in the mirror as they moved over her breasts, beginning their circular caress, rendering her completely helpless. It was too much. She was already wet between her legs before one of his hands strayed and began to caress her there, the fingers gentle and expert. She was close to the edge when finally she found enough strength to twist herself around to face him, to push him away. But when her hands came up to his chest, they betrayed her, unbuttoning his shirt, desperate to gain access to his skin.

He actually trembled when his mouth finally found hers. She hesitated. His mouth urged her on until she couldn't stand it any longer and kissed him back with the same urgency. She was gasping for air when his mouth left hers and made its way to her neck and then down to her breasts, sucking at her nipples through the cotton of the jersey and sending a jolt so powerful she clung to the dresser top.

"Oh, God, Nick," she gasped. She needed to stop, couldn't stop. The room was spinning again. Her ears ringing. No, it wasn't her ears. It was the phone.

"Nick…the phone," she managed.

He was kneeling in front of her. He stopped and looked up, his hands on her waist, his eyes filled with desire.

She pulled away from him and stumbled to the nightstand, knocking the phone and grabbing the receiver as the base crashed to the floor.

"Yes? This is Maggie O'Dell."

"Maggie, oh, thank God I got hold of you. This is Christine Hamilton. I don't know what to do. I'm sorry I'm calling so late. I tried to get hold of Nicky, but no one knows where he is."

"Christine, what's wrong?"

"It's Timmy. He wasn't here when I got home. I thought he just went home with one of his friends. But I've called. No one has seen him since this afternoon. They all went sledding on Cutty's Hill. The other kids said they saw him walking home. That was over five hours ago. I'm so scared."

Christine watched her father pace her living room. At first, when she called Nick's and her father answered, she was surprised and relieved. But now there was no comfort in watching him stomp back and forth while he barked orders to the deputies who filled her house and yard.

"Why don't you go lie down, honey? Get some rest," her father said in one of his passes. She shook her head, unable to answer.

When Nick and Maggie shoved their way into the crowded living room, Christine jumped up and almost ran to her brother. Nick pulled her to him and wrapped his strong arms around her without saying a word. He eased her back to the sofa, keeping an arm around her.

"Are you sure there isn't some place or someone you haven't checked?" Nick asked.

"I've called everyone. They all said the same thing—that he was headed for home after sledding."

"Could he have stopped somewhere on the way?" Maggie asked.

"I don't know. Other than the church, there's only houses between Cutty's Hill and here. I tried calling the rectory, but never got an answer." She saw them exchange a glance. "What? What is it?"

"Nothing," Nick said, but she knew it was something. "Maggie and I were at the rectory earlier. I'm going to check what Dad has my men doing. I'll be right back."

Maggie took off her jacket and sat next to her. The impeccable

Agent O'Dell wore a faded, stretched-out football jersey and blue jeans. Her hair was tousled and her skin flushed.

"Did I get you out of bed?" Christine asked. She was surprised to see her question embarrassed Maggie.

"Actually, I was on my way home…home to Virginia. My flight was delayed. I checked in all my luggage." She glanced at her watch. "It's probably somewhere over Chicago about now."

"You can borrow something of mine, if you like."

Maggie hesitated. Christine was sure she would decline, when Maggie said, "Are you sure you don't mind?"

"Not at all. Come on."

Christine led Maggie to her bedroom, surprised that her body had any energy left and suddenly relieved to have something to do.

Thursday, October 30

Sunlight streaked in through the rotted slats, waking Timmy up. At first, he didn't remember where he was, then he smelled the kerosene and the musty walls. The chain clanked as he sat up. His body ached from being curled up into the plastic sled.

In the sunlight he noticed the posters that covered the cracked and peeling walls. They looked like ones he had in his room back home. There were several Nebraska Cornhuskers, a *Batman* and two different *Star Wars*. The wind whistled in through the cracks, rattling the broken glass.

If he could just reach the window, he was sure he could pull the boards off. The window was small, but he could fit through and maybe call for help. He tried to shove the bed, but the heavy metal frame wouldn't budge.

He stuffed a few of the French fries into his mouth. They were cold, but salty. Under the crate he found two Snickers bars, a bag of Cheetos and an orange. He devoured the orange and candy bars and started on the Cheetos while he examined the chain that connected him to the bedpost. The links were metal with a paper-thin slit in each, but it was impossible to pull any of them apart, not even to slip just one through the slit. It was useless. He wasn't strong enough.

He heard footsteps outside the door. He scrambled up into the bed, crawling beneath the covers as the locks whined and the door screeched open.

The man came in slowly. He was bundled in a thick ski jacket, the black rubber boots and a stocking cap over the rubber mask that covered his entire head.

"Good morning," he mumbled. He set down a brown paper sack, but this time didn't remove his coat or boots. "I brought you some things."

Timmy came to the edge of the bed, showing his interest and pretending not to be frightened.

The man handed him several comic books, old ones, but in good condition. He also handed him a stack of baseball cards, secured with a rubber band. Then he started unpacking some groceries and filling the crate where Timmy had found the candy bars. He watched as the man pulled out Cap'n Crunch cereal, more Snickers bars, corn chips and several cans of SpaghettiOs.

"I tried to get some of your favorite food."

"Thanks," Timmy found himself saying out of habit. The man nodded, the eyes sparkling as though he was smiling.

"How did you know I love Cap'n Crunch?"

"I just remember things. I can't stay. Is there anything else I can get you?"

Timmy watched him extinguish the kerosene lamp and felt a twinge of panic.

"Will you be back before dark? I hate being in the dark."

The man dug in his pockets, pulling out something shiny.

"I'll leave my lighter, just in case I don't get back. But be careful, Timmy. You don't want to start a fire." He tossed the shiny metal lighter next to Timmy on the bed. Then he left.

Timmy picked up the lighter and ran his fingers over the smooth finish. He noticed the logo stamped on the side of it. He recognized the dark brown crest. He had seen it many times on the jackets and uniforms his grandfather and Uncle Nick wore. It was the symbol for the sheriff's department.

The smell of coffee nauseated Maggie, though it seemed to be the only thing to combat the effects of the Scotch. She picked at the scrambled eggs and toast while she watched the door of the diner. Nick had gone to see Judge Murphy. He said it would take only ten to fifteen minutes. That was an hour ago. The small diner was beginning to fill with its breakfast rush.

Finally, Nick came in. He was dressed in his usual uniform of jeans and cowboy boots, only this time under his unzipped jacket he wore a red Nebraska Cornhuskers sweatshirt. He looked even more handsome than she remembered.

He slid into the booth opposite her. "Judge Murphy is stalling on the search warrant for the rectory," he said quietly as he looked at the menu. "He didn't have a problem with the pickup, but he thinks—"

"Hi, Nick. What can I get for you?"

"Oh, hi, Angie. Could I just get some coffee and toast?"

"Wheat toast, right? And lots of cream with the coffee?"

"Yeah, thanks." He looked anxious for her to leave.

She smiled and left the table without even noticing Maggie, though before Nick's arrival she had filled her coffee cup three times. Maggie had watched the exchange between them, and knew immediately that the woman wasn't used to just taking Nick's diner orders.

"An old friend?" she asked, knowing she had no right to.

"Who, Angie? Yeah, I guess you could say that." He dug

Christine's cellular phone from his jacket pocket, set it on the table, then twisted out of his jacket.

"I hate these things," he said, referring to the phone, and trying to change the subject. "But Christine thought—"

"She seems very nice," persisted Maggie, glancing towards Angie.

His eyes met hers. "She is nice, but she doesn't make my palms sweaty and my knees weak like you do," he said quietly.

She looked away and concentrated on putting butter on her cold toast as though suddenly hungry.

"Look, Nick, about last night… I think it's best if we just forget it ever happened."

"What if I don't want to forget? Maggie, I haven't felt like that in a long time. I can't…"

"Please, Nick, you don't have to feed me some line…"

"It's not a line. Yesterday when I thought you were leaving and I'd never see you again, I felt as if someone had punched me in the gut. And then last night. Jesus, Maggie, you turn me inside out."

"We've been spending a lot of time together. We were both exhausted."

"I wasn't exhausted. And neither were you."

She stared at him. Had it been that obvious how much she had wanted him?

"I am married, Nick. It may not be the best marriage in the world, but it still means something. Please, let's just forget about last night."

"Here's your toast and coffee," Angie interrupted, and Maggie found no relief in ending the subject. Maybe she didn't want to forget it, either.

Angie set the plate and cup in front of Nick.

"Can I get you anything else?" she asked him.

"Maggie, do you need anything?" He purposely drew attention to Maggie, and Angie immediately looked embarrassed.

"No, thanks," said Maggie and Angie left them.

There was an awkward moment of silence. When Nick resumed the conversation, he confined himself to the business in hand.

"Father Keller told me last night that Ray Howard left the seminary last year. While I was waiting on Judge Murphy I did some checking. Howard was at a seminary in Silver Lake, New Hampshire. It's just across the border from Maine and less than five hundred miles from Wood River."

"How long was he there?"

"The last three years."

"Well, that rules him out on the Wood River murder."

"Maybe, but after three years in the seminary, he should know a little about administering last rites."

"Was he here during the first murders?"

"I'm having Hal check it out. But I did talk to the head guy at the seminary. Father Vincent wouldn't give me the details, but he did say Howard was asked to leave due to improper conduct."

"Improper conduct at a seminary could be anything from breaking a vow of silence to spitting on the sidewalk. I don't know, Nick. Howard just doesn't seem sharp enough to pull this off."

"Maybe that's what he wants everyone to believe."

"Both Howard and Keller would have had the opportunity to get rid of Father Francis," Maggie went on.

"If it wasn't an accident," Nick reminded her. "Let's get out of here." He threw a wad of bills on to the table and wrestled back into his jacket.

"Where are we going?"

"I need to impound a pickup, and you need to apologize to Father Keller."

“Sheriff Morrelli, Agent O’Dell. This is a surprise.”

“Can we come in for a few minutes, Father?” Nick rubbed his hands together to ward off the cold. Although the sun had made its first appearance in days, the piles of snow and sharp wind kept the temperature well below freezing.

Father Keller hesitated. At first, Nick thought he’d protest as he glanced at Maggie, checking to see if it was safe to let her in. Then he smiled and moved away from the door, leading them into the living room where a fire blazed.

“I’m not sure how I can be of help to the two of you. Last night—”

“Actually, Father Keller,” Maggie interrupted. “I wanted to apologize for last night. I had a bit too much to drink, and I’m afraid I get somewhat antagonistic. I hope you understand and accept my apology.”

“Of course, I understand. And I’m relieved to know it wasn’t anything I did.”

Nick watched the priest’s face. Maggie’s apology relaxed him. Even his hands dropped to his sides, no longer wringing behind his back.

“I was just about to make myself some tea. Can I get some for the two of you?”

“We are here on official business, Father Keller,” Nick said.

“Official business?”

Nick pulled the warrant from his jacket pocket and began unfolding it, while he said, "Last night we noticed the old pickup you have out back."

"Pickup?"

"The one in the trees. It matches the description a witness gave of a pickup she saw Danny Alverez get into the day he disappeared."

"I don't know how well it runs. I think Ray uses it when he goes to chop wood by the river."

Nick handed Father Keller the warrant. "Like I told you last night," he said calmly, "I'm just trying to follow up on as many leads as possible. Do you have the keys, Father?"

"The keys?"

"To the pickup?"

"I can't imagine that it's locked. Let me put on a coat and some boots, and I'll go with you."

Nick watched the priest go to the side of the fireplace and slip on the pair of rubber boots he had noticed last night. So, they were his boots. The three of them started for the door. Suddenly, Maggie grabbed on to a small table and doubled over.

"Oh, God. I think I'm going to be sick again."

"Maggie, are you okay?" Nick glanced at Father Keller and whispered, "She's been like this all morning."

"Could I use your restroom?" Maggie asked Father Keller.

"Oh, sure. Down the hall, second door on the right."

"Thanks. I'll catch up with you guys."

"Will she be okay?" Father Keller asked.

"She'll be fine. Believe me, you don't want to be too close. Earlier she made a mess all over my boots."

The priest grimaced, then followed Nick outside to the back of the rectory.

Drifts encased the pickup, forcing them to shovel a path and dig out the old metal heap. The door stuck, then creaked, metal grinding against metal, as Nick jerked it open. A musty, pent-up smell hit Nick's nostrils. The cab looked as though it had been closed up and unused for years. Disappointment stabbed at Nick. Still, he crawled into the cab with the flashlight and absolutely no clue as to what he was looking for.

He lay on the cracked, vinyl seat, then stretched and twisted his arm, allowing his hand to blindly search under the seats.

"I can't imagine there being anything but rats in this old heap," Father Keller said, standing outside the door.

Nick punched the glove compartment open and blasted the dark hole with the flashlight.

A yellowed owner's manual, a rusted can of WD-40, several McDonald's napkins, a matchbook from some place called the Pink Lady, a folded schedule with addresses and codes he didn't recognize and a small screwdriver. He palmed the matchbook. Before he closed the compartment he ran his fingers back behind the contents in the deep groove. He felt something small, smooth and round, pinched it out of the groove and palmed it with the matchbook. He slipped both items into his coat pocket after checking to make sure he was out of Father Keller's line of vision. As he started to close the compartment he noticed handwritten notes scrawled on the folded schedule. He grabbed the paper and tucked it up his sleeve. Then he slammed the compartment shut.

"Nothing here," he said, slipping the paper down into his pocket. He slid across the vinyl seat, and climbed out.

"Sorry you wasted your time," Father Keller said as he turned toward the rectory.

"Actually, I still have the bed to search."

The priest stopped, hesitated, then turned back.

Maggie checked the window again. Nick and Father Keller were still at the pickup. She continued her search down the long hall, peeking into every unlocked room. Finally, she came across a bedroom.

The room was plain and small with a wooden floor and white walls. A simple crucifix hung above the twin bed. In the corner sat a small table with two chairs. Another stand sat in the opposite corner with an old toaster and teapot. An ornate lamp sat on the nightstand.

She turned to leave, and immediately three framed prints on the wall next to the door caught her eye. They hung side by side and were prints of Renaissance paintings. Each one depicted the bloody torture of a man. Upon closer inspection she read the small print beneath each.

The Martyrdom of Saint Sebastian, 1475, Antonio Del Pollaivolo, showed a bound Saint Sebastian tied to a pedestal with arrows being shot into his body. The *Martyrdom of Saint Erasmus, 1629,* Nicolas Poussin, included winged cherubs hovering above a crowd of men who had one man stretched out and chained down while they pulled out his entrails.

Maggie wondered why anyone would want such artwork on their bedroom walls. She glanced at the last print. *The Martyrdom of Saint Hermione, 1512,* Matthias Anatello, showed a man tied to a tree while his accusers slashed at his body with knives and machetes. On the tortured man's chest were several bloody slashes, two perfect diagonals intersecting to create a jagged cross, or, from Maggie's angle, a skewed X. Yes, of course. Now it made sense. The carving on each boy's chest wasn't an X at all. It was a cross. And the cross was part of his ritual, a mark, a symbol. Did he think he was making martyrs of the boys?

She heard footsteps. They were close and getting closer. She hurried into the hall just as Ray Howard turned the corner. She startled him, but he still noticed her hand on the doorknob.

"You're that FBI agent," he said.

"Yes, I'm here with Sheriff Morrelli."

"What were you doing in Father Keller's room?"

"Oh, is this Father Keller's room? Actually, I need to use the bathroom, and I can't seem to find it."

"That's because it's way down on the other end of the hall."

"Really? Thanks." She made her way down the hall, stopping in front of the correct door and glancing back at him. "Is this it?"

"Yes."

"Thanks again." She went in. When she peeked out again, she saw Ray Howard disappear into Father Keller's bedroom.

The bed of the pickup was filled with snow, but Nick crawled up over the tailgate.

"Could you hand me the shovel, Father?"

"Oh, sure." He made his way to the tree where they had left it. "I can't imagine there being anything of use to you."

"I guess we'll see."

Nick started digging. He scooped small shovelfuls for fear of tossing evidence over the side. The handmade wooden stockracks creaked and whined against the wind gusts. The cold sliced through Nick's jacket.

Suddenly, the shovel struck something hard beneath the snow. The dull sound alerted Father Keller who approached the tailgate, close enough to look down into the hole Nick had created.

Carefully, Nick dug around the object. He tossed the shovel aside and dropped to his knees. With his hands he brushed and wiped and scooped at the snow, feeling the edges of the object, but still not able to determine what it was. Finally, Nick could see what looked like skin. His heart raced. His hands frantically pulled and chipped at the ice. A huge chunk broke away, and Nick jerked backward.

"Jesus," he said, feeling his stomach lurch.

Encased in the snow tomb was a dead dog, its black fur peeled away, its skin carved and shredded, and its throat slashed.

Nick and Father Keller stomped their way up the steps just as Maggie came out the front door of the rectory.

"Are you feeling any better?" Father Keller asked.

"Much. Thank you."

"It's a good thing you didn't come with us," Nick said, still feeling sick to his stomach. Who could do something like that to a defenseless dog? Then he felt ridiculous. It was obvious who had done it.

"Why? What did you find?"

"I'll tell you about it later."

"Would the two of you like some tea now?" Father Keller offered.

"No, thanks. We need—"

"Yes, actually," Maggie interrupted Nick. "Perhaps that might settle my stomach. That is, if it's not an inconvenience?"

"Of course not. Come in."

They followed the priest into the living room. Father Keller disappeared around the corner, and Nick joined Maggie in front of the fire.

"What's going on?" he whispered.

"Do you have Christine's cellular?"

"It's in my jacket pocket. In the hall."

"Could you please get it?"

He stared at her, waiting for some explanation, but instead she squatted in front of the fire. When he came back with the phone, she was poking through the ashes with a poker.

"What are you doing?"

"I could smell something earlier. It smelled like burnt rubber."

"Whatever it was, it's ashes now."

"Cream, lemon, sugar?" Father Keller came round the corner with a full tray. He set it down on the bench in front of the window.

"Lemon, please," Maggie answered casually.

"Cream and sugar for me," said Nick.

"If you two will excuse me, I need to make a phone call," Maggie said suddenly.

"There's a phone in the office down the hall." Father Keller pointed.

"Oh, no, thanks. I'll just use Nick's cellular. May I?"

Nick handed her the phone. She went back toward the foyer for privacy while Father Keller handed Nick a steaming cup of tea.

A phone began ringing, muffled but insistent. Father Keller looked puzzled, then headed quickly for the hallway.

"What on earth are you doing, Agent O'Dell?"

Nick followed the priest in time to see Maggie with the cellular phone to her ear as she walked down the hall, stopping and listening at each door. Father Keller followed close behind, questioning her and receiving no answers.

"What exactly are you doing, Agent O'Dell?" He tried to get in front of her, but she squeezed past.

Nick jogged down the hall.

"What's going on, Maggie?"

The muffled ringing of a phone continued, the sound getting closer and closer. Finally, Maggie pushed open the last door on the left, and the sound became crisp and clear.

"Whose room is this?"

Father Keller seemed paralyzed. He looked confused.

"Father Keller, would you please get the phone?" she asked politely, leaning against the doorjamb, careful not to enter. "It sounds as if it's in one of those drawers."

The priest didn't move. Then Nick realized that Maggie had called the number. He saw Christine's cellular phone in Maggie's hand, the buttons lit up and blinking with each ring of the hidden phone.

"Father Keller, please get the phone," she instructed again.

"This is Ray's room. I don't believe it's proper for me to go through his things."

"Just get the phone, please. It's a small, black flip-style."

He stared at her, then finally went into the room. Within seconds the ringing stopped. He came back out and handed her the small black cellular phone. She tossed it to Nick.

"Where is Mr. Howard, Father Keller?" she said. "He needs to come down to the sheriff's department with us to answer some questions."

"He's probably cleaning the church. I'll go get him."

Nick waited until Father Keller was out of sight.

"What's going on, Maggie? Why are you suddenly convinced we need to question Howard? And what's with calling his cell phone? How the hell did you even know his number?"

"I didn't dial his number, Nick. I dialed my cellular phone number. That's not his phone. It's mine. It's the one I lost in the river."

"Am I under arrest?" Ray Howard wanted to know while fidgeting in the hard-backed chair.

Maggie stared at him. His eyes bulged out—eyes a dull, watery gray with red veins telegraphing his exhaustion. She rubbed her own exhaustion from the back of her neck. She tried to remember when she had slept last.

The small conference room in the police department hummed with the percolating of coffee, filling the room with its aroma. A stream of orange sunset seeped in through the dusted blinds. She and Nick had been here for hours, asking the same questions and getting the same answers. Even though she'd insisted they bring Howard in for questioning, she still believed he wasn't the killer. Nothing had changed, but she hoped he might know something, anything, and break under pressure. Nick, however, persisted, convinced Howard was their man.

"No, Ray, you're not under arrest," Nick finally answered.

"You can only hold me here for a certain number of hours."

"And how do you know that, Ray?"

"Hey, I watch *Homicide* and *NYPD Blue*. I know my rights. And I have a friend who's a cop."

"Really? You have a friend?"

"Nick," Maggie cautioned. She noticed his impatience boiling close to the surface.

"Ray, would you like some of this fresh coffee?" she asked politely.

The well-dressed janitor hesitated, then nodded. "I use cream and two teaspoons of sugar. Real cream. If you have it."

"How about something to eat? I know we kept you over lunch, and it's almost dinnertime. Nick, perhaps you could order all of us something from Wanda's."

Ray Howard sat up, delighted. "I love Wanda's chicken-fried steak."

"Great. Nick, would you please order Mr. Howard a chicken-fried steak?"

"With mashed potatoes and brown gravy, not the white," Howard added.

"And what for you, Agent O'Dell?" Nick asked.

"A ham and cheese sandwich. I believe you know how I like it." She smiled at him, pleased when his dark-bristled jaw relaxed and his eyes softened.

"Yes, I do. I'll be right back."

She set a steaming mug of coffee in front of Howard. He reminded her of a lizard with slow deliberate blinks while he tested the hot coffee with a long pointed tongue.

"You know where Timmy Hamilton is, don't you, Ray?"

"No, I don't. And I don't know how that phone got in my drawer. I've never seen it before."

She came around the table and sat down directly across from him.

"Sheriff Morrelli thinks you killed Danny Alverez and Matthew Tanner."

"I didn't kill nobody."

"I believe you, Ray."

"You do?"

"I don't think you killed those boys."

"Good, 'cause I didn't."

"But I think you know more than you're telling us. I think you know where Timmy is."

He didn't protest, but his eyes darted around the room—the lizard looking for an escape.

"If you tell us, we can help you, Ray. But if we find out you knew and didn't tell us, well, you could end up going to jail for a long time, even if you didn't kill those boys. Where's Timmy, Ray?"

"I don't know where any kid is!" he yelled, holding the anger behind clenched, yellow teeth. "And just because I drive the pickup sometimes to cut wood doesn't mean nothing."

"Where do you go to cut wood, Ray?"

"Out by the river. The church still owns a piece of property. Out where the old St Margaret's is. It was a beautiful little church. It's falling apart now. I get lots of dried-out elm and walnut. Some oak. There's tons of river maples. The walnut burns the best." He stopped and stared out the window.

Maggie followed his empty gaze. The sun sank behind the snow-covered horizon, blood-red against the white. Cutting wood had reminded him of something, but what?

Yes, Ray Howard knew much more than he was letting on, and neither the threat of jail nor the promise of Wanda's chicken-fried steak would get him to talk. They were going to have to let him go.

Nick hung up the phone and sat back in his office chair. He realized that Maggie must have seen how badly he wanted to hit something, maybe even Ray Howard. How could she remain so cool and calm?

They were running out of time.

Aaron Harper and Eric Paltrow had been murdered less than two weeks apart. Matthew Tanner was taken exactly a week after Danny Alverez. It was only several days since Matthew, and now Timmy. The timetable grew shorter. Something was making the killer explode, sending him over the edge. And if they didn't catch him, would he simply disappear again for six years? If it wasn't Howard or Keller, who the hell was it?

Nick grabbed the crumpled paper from his desktop. The obscure schedule he had found in the pickup's glove compartment had a strange grocery list scrawled on the back. He scanned the items one more time, trying to make sense of them: wool blanket, kerosene, matches, oranges, Snickers bars, SpaghettiOs, rat poison. Perhaps it was a simple camping-trip list, yet something told Nick it was more.

There was a knock on the door, and Hal came in without waiting for an invitation.

"What do you have, Hal?"

He sank into the chair on the other side of the desk. "The empty glass vial you found in the pickup contained ether."

"Ether? Where in the world did it come from?"

"More than likely the hospital. I checked with the director, and he said they have similar vials down in the morgue. They use it as some sort of solvent, but it could be used to knock someone out. All it takes is a couple whiffs."

"Who would have access to the morgue?"

"Anyone, really. They don't lock the door."

"You're kidding?"

"Think about it, Nick. The morgue's hardly ever used, and when it is, who's gonna want to mess around down there?"

"Were you able to get any prints off the vial?"

"Just yours."

"What about the matchbook?"

"The Pink Lady is a small bar and grill in downtown Omaha, about a block from the police station. Evidently a lot of police officers hang out there. Eddie says they serve the best burgers in town."

"Eddie?"

"Yeah, Gillick was with the OPD before he moved here. I thought you knew that. 'Course, it's been a while…six or seven years now."

"I don't trust him," Nick blurted out, then regretted it as soon as he saw Hal's face.

"Eddie? Why in the world wouldn't you trust Eddie?"

"I don't know. Forget I said anything."

"You know, Nick, I don't want you to take this the wrong way, but there's a lot of people in this department who feel the same way about you."

"What way is that?" Nick sat up.

"Look, Nick, I'm your friend, and I'm with you every step of the way. But I have to tell you, some of the guys aren't too sure. They think you're letting O'Dell run the show."

There it was—the slap he had been expecting for days. He wiped a hand across his jaw as if to erase the sting.

"I guess I figured as much, especially since my dad seems to be running his own investigation."

"That's another thing. Did you know he has Eddie and Lloyd tracking down this Mark Rydell guy?"

"Rydell? Who the hell's Rydell?"

"I think he was a friend or partner of Jeffreys."

"Jesus. Doesn't anybody get it? Jeffreys didn't kill all three—" He stopped when he saw Christine standing in the doorway.

"Relax, Nick. I'm not here as a reporter." She hesitated, then came in. Her hair was a tangled mess, her eyes red, her face tear-stained. She looked like hell. "I need to do something. You have to let me help."

"Can I get you some coffee, Christine?" Hal asked.

"Yes, thanks. That would be nice."

Hal glanced back at Nick as if looking to be excused, then left.

"Come, sit down," Nick said.

"Corby gave me a temporary leave of absence with pay from the newspaper. Of course, that was only after he made sure the *Journal* would have the exclusive on whatever happens."

She struggled out of her coat, tossing it carelessly onto a chair in the corner and only staring at it when it slid to the floor. Then she paced in front of his desk, though she didn't seem to have the energy to even stand.

"Any luck tracking down Bruce?" he asked. She avoided his eyes, but he already knew it was a touchy subject that his sister had no clue as to where her ex-husband was.

"Not yet, but maybe he'll hear about Timmy on the news and get in touch with us." She grimaced. "I need to do something, Nick. I can't just sit at home and wait. What are you doing with that?" She pointed at the grocery list of items, which he'd turned over so that the strange schedule with its bizarre codes faced up.

"You know what this is?" Nick asked.

"Sure, I'm a newspaper woman, remember. It's a bundle label."

"A what?"

"A bundle label. The carriers get one each day with their newspapers. See, it shows the route number, the carrier's code number, how many papers there are to deliver, what inserts—if any—and the starts and stops."

Nick jumped out of his chair and came around to her side of the desk.

"Can you tell whose it is and what day it's for?"

"It looks like it was for Sunday, October 19. The carrier's code is ALV0436. From the addresses listed on the starts and stops, it looks like…" The realization swept over her face. She looked up at Nick with wide eyes. "This is Danny Alverez's route. It's for the Sunday he disappeared!"

When darkness came, it came quickly. Despite Timmy's efforts to remain calm, the prospect of the long, dark night ahead destroyed his defenses. He had spent the day trying to come up with an escape plan or at least a way to send a distress signal. It certainly wasn't as easy as they made it look in the movies.

The stranger had brought him *Flash Gordon* and *Superman* comic books. Yet, even equipped with the knowledge and secrets of all those superheroes, Timmy still couldn't escape.

It was too hard to think with the dark swallowing up corners of the room. He could see that the lantern had very little kerosene left, so he needed to hold off lighting it for as long as possible. But already the panic crawled over him in shivers.

He considered the kerosene heater. Perhaps he could drain kerosene from it for the lantern. Gusts of wind still knocked at the boarded window, rattling slats and sneaking through the cracks. Without the heater he might freeze before morning. No, as much as he hated to admit it, he needed the heater more than he needed the light.

All day he forced himself to listen for voices, for barking dogs or car engines, for church bells or emergency sirens. Other than a distant train whistle and one jet overhead, he had heard nothing. Where in the world was he?

He had even tried yelling until his throat hurt, only to be answered by violent gusts of wind, scolding him.

Something skidded across the floor, a click-click of tiny nails on the wood. His heart pounded. He flicked on the lighter, but couldn't see anything. Finally, he gave in. Without leaving the bed, he reached over to the crate and lit the lantern. Immediately its yellow glow filled the room. He curled up into a tight ball, pulling the covers to his chin. And for the first time since his dad had left town, Timmy allowed himself to cry.

She was smart. Definitely a worthy adversary. But he wondered how much Special Agent Maggie O'Dell really knew and how much was just a game. It didn't matter. He enjoyed games. They took his mind off the throbbing.

No one noticed him as he walked down the sterile hallways. Those who did nodded and scurried past. His presence was accepted here as easily as anywhere in the community. He took the stairs. Today even the stairwells smelled of ammonia, immaculately scrubbed.

The door slammed shut behind him. He had been here before and found comfort in the familiar surroundings. Somewhere above, a fan wheezed. Otherwise there was silence, appropriate silence for this temporary tomb.

He snapped on the surgical gloves. Which will it be? Drawer number one, two or three? Perhaps four or five? He chose number three, pulling and wincing at the scrape of metal, but pleased to see he had been correct.

The black body bag looked so small on the long silver bed. He unzipped it carefully, reverently, tucking and folding it to the sides of the small gray body. The coroner's surgical wounds—precise slices and cuts—disgusted him, as did the puncture marks he himself had administered. Matthew's poor little body resembled a road map. Matthew, however, was gone—to a much better place. Someplace free of pain and humiliation. Free of loneliness and abandonment. Yes, he had seen to it that Matthew's eternal rest would be peaceful. He could remain an innocent child forever.

He unwrapped the fillet knife, setting it to the side. He needed to destroy the one piece of evidence that could link him to the murders. How careless he had been. How insanely stupid. Maybe it was too late, but if that were true Maggie O'Dell would now be reading him his rights.

He unzipped the body bag farther until he could examine Matthew's small legs. Yes, there it was on the thigh, the purple teeth marks. The result of the demon's rage inside him. Shame burned down into his stomach, liquid and hot. He moved the boy's leg and picked up the knife.

Yes, he was getting reckless. It was becoming harder and harder to clean up after himself, to stifle that hideous demon that sometimes got in the way of his mission. Even now, as he gripped the knife, he couldn't bring himself to cut. His hand shook. Sweat dripped from his forehead into his eyes. But soon it would be over.

Soon, Sheriff Nick Morrelli would have his prime suspect. He had already made sure of that, laying the groundwork and planting enough evidence, just enough clues. He was getting good at it. And it was so easy, exactly as it had been with Ronald Jeffreys. All it had taken with Jeffreys was an assortment of items in Jeffreys' trunk and an anonymous phone call to the supersheriff, Antonio Morrelli. But he had been reckless even then, including Eric Paltrow's underpants in Jeffreys' treasure chest of incriminating items.

He had always taken each boy's underpants for his own souvenir, but with Eric he had forgotten. It had been easy to retrieve them from the morgue. His mistake, however, had been including Eric's and not Aaron's underpants among the items he had planted in Jeffreys' trunk. Curiously, he had never known if his blunder had gone unnoticed or if the great and powerful Antonio Morrelli simply chose to ignore it. But he would not chance it this time. He would not be reckless. And soon he would be able to put the throbbing to a stop, maybe for good. Just a few loose ends to tie up and one more lost boy to save. Then his demons could rest.

Yes, poor Timmy would finally be saved. So many bruises he could only imagine what the boy had to endure at the hands of those who claimed to love him. And he did like the boy, but then, he had liked them all, chosen them carefully and saved each and every one of them. Delivered them from evil.

Christine pushed the copier button and watched Timmy's toothy grin slide out into the tray. He'd hate that she was using last year's school photo. She wondered if the task simply kept her out of Nick's way. He insisted the more photos they got out to the news media and store owners, the better chance of triggering someone's memory.

She felt him standing behind her. The smell of his aftershave lotion assaulted her. She turned slowly just as Eddie Gillick pressed in close against her, trapping her between the copy machine and his body. Sweat beads gathered on his lip above the thin mustache. He was breathing hard as though he had just come in running.

"Excuse me, Christine. I just need to make a couple of copies of these photos." He flashed them at her. When she only glanced, he held them up to her, slowly shuffling them one after another. Glossy eight-by-tens, the brilliant color emphasized the red gashes. A close-up of skin peeled back. A throat slashed. And Matthew Tanner's pale face, his glassy eyes staring out at her.

Christine squeezed past, scraping her shin on the copy machine's stand in order to escape Eddie Gillick. He watched, smiling at her as she bumped into a state trooper, smashed a knee into a desk and finally made it across the room. Safe in the corner next to the watercooler, she stared out at the chaos. Were they all moving in slow motion, or was it just her imagination? The room moved. A slight tip to one side. No one else seemed to notice. Then a slight tip to the other. She felt her body sliding down the wall. Then someone shut off the lights.

Nick came out of his office just in time to see a crowd gathered around the watercooler. He saw Christine slumped on the floor. Lucy fanned her with a file folder, while Hal held her up against his shoulder. Nick's father looked on with the rest, his hands deep in his pockets. Nick knew what he was thinking. How dared Christine show such weakness in front of his colleagues?

"What happened?" Nick asked Eddie Gillick at the copy machine.

"Don't know. Didn't see it happen," Eddie said as he pressed the copier's buttons, his back turned to the commotion.

At least Christine looked conscious now. Hal helped her to her feet. Adam Preston handed her a paper cup, and she gulped water as if they had pulled her out of the desert. Then Lucy put her arm round her waist and led her out of the office.

"Okay, everybody," his father announced. "Show's over. Let's get back to work."

When he saw Nick, he waved him over. Nick stood firm. His father signed something for Lloyd, then wandered over, completely oblivious to Nick's defiance.

"Lloyd's found Rydell. We're bringing him in for questioning."

"You have no authority to do that," Nick replied.

"Excuse me?"

"You no longer have the authority to bring anyone in for questioning."

"I'm trying to help you, boy, so you don't look like a fucking idiot to the whole goddamn community."

"Mark Rydell had nothing to do with any of this."

"Right. You're placing your money on some gimpy church janitor."

"I have evidence that implicates Ray Howard. What do you have on Rydell?"

By now the office had come to a standstill again.

"Rydell's a known fag. Has a rap sheet as long as my arm. He was Jeffreys' fag for a while. I'd bet the farm that he's your copy-cat killer. Only you can't see it 'cause you can't see beyond Agent Maggie's cute little ass."

The heat crawled up Nick's neck. His father turned away from him. Nick glanced around. He saw Maggie in the doorway to the conference room. His eyes met hers. In an instant, he knew she had heard.

"This isn't a copycat killer," he said to his father's back.

"What the fuck are you talking about now?"

"Jeffreys was only responsible for Bobby Wilson's death. He didn't kill all three boys. But then, you already knew that."

"What the fuck are you implying?"

"I've read Jeffreys' arrest file. I've seen all the autopsy reports. There's no way in hell Jeffreys committed all three murders. Jeffreys told you that, over and over again."

"Oh, so now you believe a goddamn murdering fag over your own father?"

"Your own reports prove Jeffreys didn't kill the other two boys. Only you were too blind. No, you wanted to be a hero. So you ignored the truth and let a killer get away. Or maybe you even helped plant the evidence. Now your own grandson's going to pay the price for your mistakes and your fucking pride."

The fist took Nick completely off guard. It slammed into his jaw and knocked him back into the copy machine. He caught his balance, but his vision was still blurred when the second fist slammed into his face. He looked up to see his father in the same place, same stance, a look of surprise on his face. Nick didn't even realize it wasn't his father's fists that had hit him until he saw Hal restraining Eddie Gillick.

Maggie wasn't surprised when Nick didn't come back to their interrogation room. Adam Preston delivered dinner from Wanda's. Maggie told Ray Howard he was welcome to stay and eat his steak, then he was free to go. She started to leave while Adam unpacked and laid out the rest of the food.

"Agent O'Dell, this is for you."

"I'm not very hungry." She turned to him, but it wasn't a sandwich he handed her. She stared at the small white envelope. "Where did you get that?"

"It was in the order from Wanda's. It has your name on it." He held it out to her, but she made no attempt to take it.

"Agent O'Dell? What is it? Do you want me to open it?"

"No, I'll take it." She opened it without hesitation. Her fingers were amazingly steady though her stomach did acrobatic flips.

She read the note. It was simple, only one line: "I KNOW ABOUT STUCKY."

She glanced up at Adam.

"Is Nick around?" She needed to keep her breathing even and steady.

"No one's seen him since Eddie decked him," said Adam.

"Eddie decked him?" Ray Howard queried. Adam nodded.

Howard smiled up at them over a forkful of mashed potatoes. "Eddie's my man," he said, then stuffed his mouth.

"What do you mean by that?" Maggie snapped at him.

"Nothin'. He's just a friend."

"Deputy Gillick is a friend of yours?"

"Yeah, he's a friend. There ain't no crime in that, is there? We do stuff together. It's no big deal."

"What kind of stuff?"

"Sometimes he comes over to the rectory and plays cards with Father Keller and me. Sometimes just him and me go out for burgers."

"You and Deputy Gillick?"

"Didn't you say I was free to go?"

She stared him down. Those clever, reptilian eyes did know more, much more. But deep down, she knew he wasn't the killer. His limp would never allow him to maneuver the steep woods along the river, let alone carry a sixty- to seventy-pound boy.

"Yes, I did say you were free to leave," she finally answered. She gestured to Adam, and he followed her out of the room. He told her what had occurred between Nick and his father, and assured her that Nick had survived Gillick's attack.

"Glad to hear it," she said with a smile. "Tell me something—you grew up in Platte City, right?"

He nodded.

"What can you tell me about the old church, the one in the country?"

"We checked it out, if that's what you mean. Lloyd and I went out there before the snow and then again after. The place is boarded up. Didn't look like anyone's been in there for years. No footprints, no tire tracks."

"It's close to the river?"

"Yeah, just off Old Church Road—guess that's probably where it gets its name. The church is listed as an historical landmark."

"How do you know all of that?"

"My dad owns land close by. He wanted to buy the church property, tear down the building. It's prime farmland. Father Keller told him it couldn't be torn down on account of it's registered as an historical landmark. I guess it was used as part of John Brown's Underground Railroad. Supposedly there's a tunnel from the church to the graveyard."

"Tell me more."

"They hid runaway slaves in the church. At night they used the tunnel to sneak them to the river where a boat would take them up-stream to the next hideout. They say the tunnel's all caved in—too close to the river. They don't even use the graveyard anymore. A few years ago when the river flooded, it uprooted some graves. Even sent a few coffins floating down the river. That was kind of a creepy sight."

Maggie imagined the swift river current sucking corpses from their graves. It sounded like the perfect place for a killer obsessed with his victims' salvation.

Maggie decided to leave Nick a note, though she had no clue what to say.

When she went in to his office, she left the lights off, using the glow from the streetlights below to guide her. She bumped her shin against a chair leg.

"Damn it," she muttered.

While bent over and rubbing her leg, she noticed Nick sitting on the floor in the corner. He was hugging his knees to his chest, in the dark, staring out the window, apparently oblivious to her presence.

Without a word, she walked over and took a place beside him on the floor. Out of the corner of her eye she saw the cracked lip, bruised and swollen. Dried blood stained that perfectly chiseled jaw.

"You know, Morrelli, for an ex-football player you fight like a girl."

There was no response. She sat quietly by his side. Minutes passed. Just as she was stretching her legs to get up, he said, "My dad was wrong to say what he did about you."

"You mean I don't have a cute little ass?"

Finally, she caught a hint of a smile.

"Okay, only half wrong."

"Don't worry about it, Morrelli. I've heard worse."

"You know," he said, "when all this began, the only thing I cared about was how I'd look, whether people would think I was incompetent."

She kept quiet.

"I am incompetent. I don't know the first thing about heading a murder investigation. Maybe if I had admitted that in the beginning…maybe Timmy wouldn't be missing."

"You've done everything possible, Nick. Believe me, if there was something I thought you should have done or should be doing differently, I certainly would have told you. If you haven't noticed, I'm not shy in that area."

Another smile.

"Whatever happens, it won't be your fault, Nick." She changed the subject while pretending to be on it. "You're doing everything possible. At some point you have to let yourself off the hook."

He looked at her. "Your nightmares," he said quietly. "You haven't let yourself off the hook about something. What is it, Maggie? Is it Stucky?"

"How do you know about Stucky?"

"That night at my house, you yelled out his name several times. I thought you'd tell me about him. When you didn't…well, I figured maybe it wasn't any of my business. Maybe it's still none of my business."

"Albert Stucky is a serial killer I helped capture a little over a month ago. We nicknamed him The Collector. He'd kidnap two, three, sometimes four women at a time, keeping them in some condemned building or abandoned warehouse. When he got tired of them, he killed them, slicing their bodies, bashing in their skulls, chewing off pieces of them."

"Jesus, I thought this guy we're chasing was screwed up."

"Stucky is certainly one of a kind. It was my profile that identified him. Over the course of two years, we tracked him. Every time we got close, he moved to another part of the country. Somewhere along the line, Stucky discovered that I was the profiler. That's when the game began."

She glanced at him. He must have bitten down on his lip. It was bleeding again.

"You're still bleeding."

He wiped a sleeve across his mouth. "What else is new? I fight like a girl. Tell me about the game."

"Stucky probed my background. Somehow he found out about my family, my father's death, my mother's alcoholism. He knew everything, or so it seemed. About a year ago I started receiving notes. He always included a piece of his victims—a finger, sometimes just a piece of skin with a birthmark or tattoo, once a nipple."

Nick shook his head but didn't say anything.

"He'd send clues as to where he was keeping the women. If I guessed right, he rewarded me with a new clue. If I guessed wrong, he punished me with a dead body. I was wrong a lot. Every time we found one of his victims in a Dumpster, I felt like it was my fault."

"We finally tracked him down in Miami. After a few clues I was almost certain I knew he was using an abandoned warehouse by the river. I dreaded being wrong. I didn't think I could handle another dead woman on my conscience. So I didn't tell anyone. I decided to check it out myself. That way, if I was wrong, no one ended up dead. Only, I was right, and Stucky was waiting for me. He ambushed me before I even saw it coming.

"He tied me to a steel post, and then he made me watch. I watched while he tortured and mutilated two women. Actually, the second one was punishment because I closed my eyes while he was bashing in the skull of the first. He had warned me that he would just keep bringing out another if I closed my eyes.

"I watched him beat and slice and rip apart two women and I felt so…so goddamn helpless. I was so close…" She rubbed her shoulders. She could still feel it. "I was so close I could feel their blood splatter me, along with pieces of their brains, chips of their bones."

"But you did get him?"

"Yes. We got him. Only because an old fisherman heard the screams and called 911. We certainly didn't get him on my account. That reminds me," she said, trying to resume normalcy. "I got another note." She dug out the crumpled envelope and handed it to Nick.

He pulled out the card, read it, and leaned back against the wall. "Jesus, Maggie. What do you suppose this means?"

"I don't know. Maybe nothing. Maybe he's just having some fun."

"So what do we do now?" said Nick, untangling his legs.

"How do you feel about raiding graveyards?"

Timmy watched the lantern's flame dance. It reminded him of the camping trips he and his dad had taken. His dad hadn't been an experienced camper. It had taken them almost two hours to set up the tent. Then Dad had melted Mom's favorite pot by leaving it in the fire too long.

He knew his mom and dad were mad at each other. But his mom had told him his dad still loved him. That he didn't want anybody to know where he was because he didn't want to pay them any money. Sometimes Timmy didn't understand grown-ups.

He brought his hands up to the lantern's glass to feel its glow. The chain attached to his ankle clinked against the metal bedpost. Suddenly, he stared at it, remembering the metal pot his dad had ruined on the campfire. The chain links weren't thick. How hot did metal need to get to bend?

He grabbed the glass, but snatched his hands back from the heat. He pulled off the pillowcase and wrapped his hands, then tried again, gently tugging the glass casing off without breaking it. The flame danced some more, reared up, then settled down. He put the pillowcase back on the pillow. Then he set the lantern on the floor in front of him and lifted his leg, grabbing a length of chain close to his ankle. He let several links dangle into the flame. He waited a few minutes, then started to pull. It wasn't working. He needed to be patient. He needed to think of something else. He kept the links in the flame. What was that song his mom was singing the other morning in the bathroom? It was from a movie. Oh yeah, *The Little Mermaid*.

"Under the sea… Darling it's better, down where it's wetter." He pulled on the chain again. Still no movement. It surprised him how many of the words he remembered. He tried out his Jamaican accent. "Under the sea."

It moved. The metal was giving. He strained, pulling as hard as he could. Yes, the slit between the two links grew little by little. Just a little more, and he could slip it through.

The footsteps outside the door sent his heart plunging. No, just a few more seconds. He pulled with all his might as the locks clanked and screeched open.

Christine tried to remember the last time she had eaten. She pulled herself up off the old couch in a back office, where Lucy had left her after she had fainted.

The door opened. Her father came in.

"Feeling better?"

"Yes, thanks. I don't think I've eaten today. I'm sure that's why I got so light-headed."

"Yep. That'll do it. I called your mother. She's trying to catch a flight later this evening. Hopefully, she'll be here by morning."

"Thanks. It'll be nice to have her here."

"Now, don't get upset, pumpkin, but I also called Bruce."

"Bruce?"

"He has a right to know. Timmy is his son."

"Yes, of course, and Nick and I have been trying to contact him. You know where he is?"

"I have a phone number for emergencies."

"So you've known all along how to contact him?"

Her father looked stunned. How dared she direct such shrill anger toward him?

"And you knew that I've been trying to find him to make him pay child support for over eight months. All this time, you've had his phone number?"

"For emergencies, Christine."

"Seeing that his son has food on the table isn't an emergency? How could you?"

"Bruce said he left you with plenty in savings."

"He left us with exactly $164.21 in our savings account and over five thousand dollars of credit-card bills."

"The son of a bitch. That's not what he told me. But you threw the man out of his own house, Christine."

"He was fucking his receptionist."

His face grew scarlet with disapproval. "Sometimes a man strays, Christine. I'm not saying it's right, but it's not a reason to throw him out of his own house."

"I wonder, would you be this forgiving if I had fucked the UPS man?"

He winced. After all, Tony Morrelli's little girl didn't fuck.

"Look, you're upset, Christine. Why don't I have one of the guys drive you home?"

She nodded, and he escaped.

After a few short minutes the door opened again, and Eddie Gillick came in.

"Your dad asked me to drive you home."

Nick rammed the Jeep into gear, picking up speed and leaving Platte City behind. He glanced at Maggie sitting quietly next to him.

He felt a sudden strength. He had to be strong for Timmy's sake, and maybe, just maybe, he could do that as long as he didn't have to do it alone. Jesus, that was a first—Nick Morrelli might actually need someone!

He could ignore the sick feeling in his gut. He would put the vision of Danny Alverez's vacant eyes out of his mind. Timmy had to be okay. It couldn't be too late. He stepped on the accelerator. Wisps of snow scampered across in spots, but the wind had died down considerably.

"Maybe you should fill me in," he said. "Why are we going to a graveyard in the middle of the night?"

"I know your men checked the old church, but what about the tunnel?"

"The tunnel? I think that caved in years ago."

"Are you sure?"

"Well, no. Actually, I've never seen it. When I was a kid we thought it was just made up. You know, to scare us, to keep us from screwing around the church at night. There were stories about bodies rising from the dead, digging themselves out of their graves and crawling through the tunnel. Finding their way back to the church to redeem their condemned souls."

"Sounds like the perfect place for a killer who believes in redemption."

"You think that's where he's keeping Timmy? In a hole in the ground?"

"It's only a hunch," she said. "At this point, I don't think we have anything to lose by checking it out. Ray Howard mentioned going there to cut wood. He knows something. Maybe he's seen something."

"I can't believe you let him go."

"He's not the killer, Nick. But I think he might know who is."

"You still think it's Keller, don't you?"

"Keller could have easily planted my cell phone in Howard's room. He had access to the pickup. He keeps those strange paintings of tortured martyrs, martyrs with the sign of the cross sliced into their chests."

"The guy has bad taste in art, that doesn't make him a killer."

"Keller also knew all three boys."

"Actually, all five boys," Nick interrupted. "Lucy was able to dig up lists and applications. Eric Paltrow and Aaron Harper did attend church camp the summer before they were murdered. But that means Ray Howard knew all the boys, too."

"It's more than that, Nick. Somehow, I think this killer believes he's making these boys martyrs, saving them from something. It's like something clicks in this guy and sends him on a mission. Father Keller fits much of that profile. Who else would administer last rites to his victims but a priest? And who else would have the perfect opportunity to push Father Francis down a flight of stairs and get away with it?"

"Jesus, Maggie. You still won't let that go?"

"Looks like I may not have a choice. The archdiocese is in charge of Father Francis' remains, since there's no next of kin, and they see no reason for an autopsy."

There was silence between them. If Father Francis had been shoved down those stairs, Nick could imagine Howard being more than capable of doing it.

"Maybe we've got this wrong," Nick said. "Maybe Keller is involved, but maybe he's protecting someone."

"What do you mean?"

"Father Francis couldn't tell us about Jeffreys' confession. Suppose the killer confessed to Father Keller?"

Maggie sat quietly. She was obviously mulling over the idea. Perhaps it wasn't so far-fetched, Nick realized.

Suddenly, out of the darkness, Maggie said, "Did you know Ray Howard and Eddie Gillick are friends?"

Christine knew it was anger at her dad that had rendered her temporarily insane. Otherwise, why would she be climbing into Eddie Gillick's rusted Chevy? Yet here she was with her feet kicking empty McDonald's containers. A spring poked into her back, and crumb-filled stuffing grew out of the cushion next to her. It smelled of French fries, cigarettes and aftershave.

Eddie slid into the driver's seat, tossing his hat into the back and stealing a long glance at himself in the rearview mirror. He stuck the key in the ignition, and the loose tailpipe set the car vibrating.

Despite her long trench coat, it felt as if something was crawling on her bare legs. She opened her coat to make sure there weren't black bugs skittering up her thighs. As she ran a hand over one leg, she noticed Eddie watching, smiling. She pulled her coat closed and decided bugs were better than Eddie's eyes.

He gunned the engine, slamming her back into the seat. She reached up for the seat belt and saw it had been cut out. He sped past the turn to her street and a fresh panic sent her hand to the door handle. It broke off with a snap, and Eddie frowned at her.

"Relax, Christine. Your dad said I should get you something to eat."

"I'm really not hungry. Really, I'm just tired."

"I can grill you up a steak that'll make your mouth water. Just happen to have a couple in my fridge."

"Maybe another time, Eddie." She made her voice as sweet as

possible, despite the revulsion. “I really am tired. Could you please just take me home?”

She watched his face out of the corner of her eye. His mustache twitched, then a crooked smile.

“You came on to me pretty strong that evening out by the river,” he said.

Big mistake. How could she have been so stupid? “Look, I’m sorry about that, Eddie. It was my first big assignment. I guess I was nervous.”

“It’s okay, Christine. I know it’s been over a year since your husband left. Hell, you don’t have to play shy with me. I know women get horny, too.”

Oh, dear God. This was not going well. She felt sick again as she watched houses pass by. A few more blocks and they’d leave streetlights behind. They were headed out of town.

“Eddie, please. My son’s missing. I’m really in awful shape. Please just take me home.”

“I know what you need, Christine. Take your mind off things for a while. Just relax.”

Her eyes darted around the car. Anything…was there anything she could use as a weapon? Then in the glow of the panel lights she saw a long-necked beer bottle roll out from under the seat, as though answering her prayer.

He was driving awfully fast. She needed to wait. Wait until they stopped, or they’d end up in a snow-filled ditch, stranded in the middle of nowhere.

“It wouldn’t hurt you to be nice to me, Christine. If you’re nice, I might just tell you where Timmy is.”

Timmy hid his feet under the covers. He scooted into the corner of the bed. Something was wrong. The stranger seemed upset. He hadn't said anything since he came into the room. Instead, he threw his ski jacket onto the bed and started pacing.

Timmy kept quiet and watched. The stranger had forgotten to close the door behind him. The smell of dirt and mold came in with a draft. It was black on the other side of the door.

"What happened to the lantern?"

"I...I couldn't light it, so I had to take that thing off. Sorry, I forgot to put it back on."

The stranger took the glass and snapped it in place. When he bent over, Timmy saw black, curly hair sticking out from under his mask. Richard Nixon. That was the dead president the mask resembled. It had taken Timmy three attempts at naming the presidents before he remembered.

Suddenly, the stranger grabbed his jacket and wrestled into it. "It's time to go."

"Where?" Timmy tried to control his excitement. Was it really possible that the stranger might take him home? Maybe he'd realized his mistake. Timmy crawled out of bed, keeping the chain behind his feet.

"Take off all your clothes, except your underpants."

"What? It's awfully cold out."

"Don't ask questions."

"But I don't understand what—"

"Just do it, you little son of a bitch."

The unexpected anger felt like a slap in the face. He mustn't cry. He wasn't a baby anymore. But he was scared. So scared his fingers shook as he untied his shoes.

"I don't understand," he mumbled again.

"You don't need to understand. Hurry up."

"I don't mind staying here."

"Shut the fuck up, you little bastard."

Tears ran down Timmy's cheeks, and he didn't bother to wipe at them. He undid his belt, remembered the chain on his ankle, then worked on his shirt buttons instead. The stranger would need to unchain him. Would he notice the bent links? Would he get even more angry? Already Timmy felt a cold draft swirling around him. His vision was blurred from the tears.

Suddenly, the stranger stood perfectly still in the middle of the room, cocking his head to one side. He was listening. Timmy strained to hear over his thumping heart. Then he heard it—a car engine in the distance, getting closer and slowing down.

"Fuck!" the stranger spat, grabbing the lantern and heading for the door.

"Please don't take the light."

"Shut the fuck up, you little crybaby."

He wheeled back around, smashing the back of his hand across Timmy's face. Timmy scrambled into the bed. He hugged the pillow, but jerked away at the sight of the red blotch.

"You better be ready when I get back," the stranger snapped. "And stop bleeding all over the place."

The stranger ran out the door, slamming it and the locks back into place, leaving Timmy in a hole of solid black. He hurried out in such a rush that he didn't even notice Timmy's chain, broken and dangling over the edge of the bed.

Christine didn't need to ask what Eddie was planning. She recognized the winding dirt road that climbed then plunged. It snaked through the towering maples and walnut trees that lined the riverbank. This was where Jason Ashford and Amy Stykes were probably headed the night they stumbled over Danny Alverez's body.

Was it possible that Eddie knew where Timmy was? Christine remembered that a church janitor had been brought in for questioning. Could Eddie have overheard something? Yet, if Nick knew something, *anything*, wouldn't he have told her? No, of course not. He'd want to keep her out of the way, to stop her writing more stories.

Eddie disgusted her. But if he knew where Timmy was… Oh, God, if she could just have Timmy back, safe and sound. What price would she be willing to pay? What price would any mother—Laura Alverez, Michelle Tanner—what price would they pay to have their sons back?

Nevertheless, when the car pulled off the road and slid into the clearing overlooking the river, the panic crawled through her, sending a shiver down her back.

Eddie cut the engine and extinguished the headlights. The dark engulfed them as though they hovered in it, looking down on black treetops, the glittering river below.

"Well, here we are," Eddie said, turning toward her expectantly, but staying behind the wheel.

Her foot found the beer bottle, and she kept it from sliding under the seat. She heard a wrapper crackle, followed by a slap.

Then a match sizzled, the smell of sulfur attacking her nostrils as he lit a cigarette.

"Mind if I have one of those?"

In the light of his cigarette, she saw the twisted smile. He handed her one, lit another match and waited for her. The match burned down close to his fingers. By the time he lit hers, he ended up scorching his fingertips.

"Damn. I hate matches. Lost my lighter someplace."

"I didn't know you smoked," she said. She inhaled, waiting, hoping the nicotine could calm her.

"I'm trying to quit."

"Me, too." She smiled at him. See, they did have something in common. She could do this, couldn't she? By now her eyes had adjusted to the dark, and she could see him. "Do you really know where Timmy is?"

"Maybe," he answered in a puff of smoke. "What are you willing to do to find out?" He moved his arm across the seat until his stubby fingers brushed her hair, then wandered across her cheek, swooping down to her neck.

"How do I know this isn't just some trick?"

"You don't."

His fingers slid under her coat collar, unbuttoning and pulling the coat open until he could see her blouse and skirt. Her skin crawled under his touch.

His fingertips brushed across her breasts. She sat perfectly still. Don't think, she told herself. Shut off. But she wanted to scream when his hand fondled her breast, squeezing her nipple, Eddie watching and smiling at it growing hard and erect under his touch.

He put out his cigarette and scooted closer, so that his other hand could assault her thigh. His stubby fingers slithered up, and she watched as they disappeared up her skirt. She refused to part her thighs for him, and he laughed, his breath sour in her face.

"Come on, Christine, relax."

"I'm just nervous." Her voice quivered and he seemed pleased. "Do you have protection?" she asked.

"Well, I don't use condoms," he declared.

"If you don't, I'm afraid we can't do this," she said.

"That's okay," he said, running the fingertips of his other hand over her lips and pushing his thumb into her mouth. "There's other things we can do!"

Her stomach lurched. Would she throw up? But she couldn't afford to make him angry.

He reached down, unzipped his trousers and pulled out his erect penis. It snaked out of his pants, long and thick. He took her hand. She snatched it away. He smiled and took it again, wrapping her fingers around him and squeezing his hand over hers until she could feel the bulging vein throbbing. He groaned and leaned back.

"Do you really know where Timmy is?" she asked one more time, trying to remind herself of her mission.

He closed his eyes and his breathing rasped. "Oh, baby, squeeze and suck me real good, and I'll tell you anything you want to hear."

At least his hands were off her. Then she remembered the cigarette in her other hand, the long ash lingering at the end. She took another draw until the end glowed red-hot. She squeezed him, digging her nails into the hard thickness.

"What the fuck!"

His eyes flew open. He grabbed for her hand. She shoved the glowing cigarette into his face. He howled, swatting at his scorched cheek. She reached around him, grabbing the door handle. His hands snapped around her wrists, immediately letting go when she slammed her knee up into his erect penis. She scooped up the beer bottle, and cracked it across his head. She scooted to her side of the seat, anchored her back against her door. She brought her knees up, and with all the strength she could gather slammed her high-heeled feet into his chest. Eddie flew out the door.

He was getting to his feet when she pulled his door shut, locking it and checking the other doors. He pounded on the glass as her fingers fumbled with the keys in the ignition. The Chevy sputtered to life.

Eddie climbed onto the hood, screaming at her and kicking at the windshield. A small crack raced across, spreading into a spiderweb. She threw the car into reverse and slammed on the accelerator. Eddie flew from the hood. He scrambled to his feet as she shifted into drive and floored it, sending gravel spitting.

The car plunged down the winding road into a hole of black. The headlights! She grabbed at knobs, sending the wipers swishing and the radio blaring. She looked down for only a second, found the knob and lit up the road, just in time to see the sharp curve. Even with both hands twisting the steering wheel, it wasn't enough. The car flew across the snow-filled ditch, through the barbed-wire fence and into a tree.

Nick watched the dark church in the rearview mirror as the Jeep bounced over the deep tire tracks, the only things identifying the deserted road.

"You sure you didn't see a light?"

Maggie glanced over the back of the seat. "Maybe it was a reflection. There is a moon out tonight."

The wood-framed church looked dark and gray, disappearing from the rearview mirror as he took the sharp turn up into the graveyard. Now to his left, he stared at the church again. It was set in the middle of a snow-covered field with tall, brown grass stabbing through the white. All the stained-glass windows had been removed or broken and boarded up. Even the huge front door was slowly rotting behind thick boards haphazardly nailed at odd diagonals.

"It looked like a light," Nick said. "In one of the basement windows."

"Why don't you check it out? I can wander around here for a while."

"I only have one flashlight." He leaned over, snapping open the glove compartment.

"That's okay, I have this." She shone the tiny penlight into his eyes.

"Oh, yeah. That should show you a lot."

She smiled.

"I can leave the headlights on."

"No, that's okay. I'll be fine," she assured him.

A fence surrounded the graveyard. The gate hung on one hinge, swinging and clicking back and forth though there was no wind. A chill slithered down Nick's back. He'd hated this place, ever since he was a kid and Jimmy Montgomery dared him to run up and touch the black angel.

It was impossible not to notice the angel, even in the dead of night. At this angle, looking up the hill, the tall stone figure hovered above the other tombstones. Its chipped wings only made it more menacing. His memory was of Halloween, almost twenty-five years ago. Then suddenly, he remembered that tomorrow was Halloween.

They reached for the door handles at the same time. Not for the first time, hers clicked, but did not function.

"Damn," he muttered. "I've got to get that fixed. Hold on."

He jumped out and hurried around to open the door for her. Then he stood silently by her side, mesmerized by the moonlight caught on the angel's face, radiating a glow almost as if from within.

"Nick, are you okay?"

"Sorry. It's just…the angel." He waved a hand at it, streaking its surface with the light from his flashlight.

"It doesn't come to life at midnight, does it?"

She was making fun. He glanced at her. Her face was serious, only adding to the sarcasm. He started walking away, heading down the road to the church. Somewhere in the distance a hoot owl tested its voice, receiving no reply.

Nick tried to stay focused, to ignore the blackness pressing against him, swallowing him with each step. It was ridiculous to let those old childhood fears creep into his gut. After all, he *had* crossed the dark cemetery that night. He had touched the angel while his friends watched, none of them attempting to follow. If he remembered correctly, the earth hadn't opened up and swallowed him, though it had felt as if it would at the time.

He plodded through the unbroken snowdrifts. He crouched at one of the basement windows and shone his light through the rotted slats. There were crates stacked on crates. Movement in the corner. His light caught a rat escaping into a hole in the wall. Rats. Jesus, he hated rats.

He made his way to the next window and suddenly heard the crack of wood. It cut through the silence. He shot light at the windows ahead of him. He expected to see something or someone smashing through the rotted wood.

Another crack, then the tinkle of broken glass. It must be around the corner. He tried running. The snow slowed his feet. He extinguished the flashlight, and pulled out his gun. The noises continued. He rushed the corner, pointing his gun into the blackness. Nothing. He snapped on the flashlight. Wood and glass lay scattered in the snow beneath a window. His light caught movement disappearing into the trees—a small, black figure and a flash of orange.

Maggie concentrated on the ground, looking for any breaks in the snow or freshly dug holes. Timmy had disappeared after the snowfall. If he was here, the snow would be disturbed. If a tunnel existed, where in the world would the entrance be?

A breeze swirled up out of the trees that lined the back of the graveyard. The huge maples were the beginnings of the thick woods that led down to the river. She tried to imagine frightened runaway slaves navigating the steep incline without the aid of flashlights or lanterns.

A flapping sound came from behind her. Maggie spun around. Something moved. The tiny penlight picked out a black shadow sprawled on the ground at the end of the rows. She approached slowly. Her hand crawled inside her jacket and rested on the butt of her revolver. She recognized the black tarp, the kind used to cover freshly dug graves. She sighed, then remembered the graveyard hadn't been used in years. Wasn't that what Adam had told her? The adrenaline started pumping.

The tarp was down the hill, close to the tree line. Only a few headstones existed on this side. The tarp looked new, no cracks or worn patches. Rocks and snow anchored the corners, but one corner flapped free, its rock set aside. Set aside, not blown aside, not by tonight's slight breeze.

She pulled the loose corner and whipped the tarp aside. She didn't need extra light to see. Underneath was a door, narrow and long, thick wood rotting around the hinges and caving in slightly in the middle.

She grabbed the edge of the door. There was no handle. She pulled and yanked until it gave way, but it was heavy, straining her muscles, splinters threatening her fingers. She dropped the door, got a better grip and tried again. This time she swung it open. The musty odor slapped her in the face. It was filled with decay, wet earth and mold.

She couldn't see beyond the third step with her penlight. It would be ridiculous to go down with such poor lighting. She pulled out her revolver. She glanced back up the hill one more time. Silence. No sign of Nick. She descended slowly into the narrow black hole.

Timmy skidded down into a prickly bush. He had heard someone close behind, felt the flash of light on his back. He didn't dare stop or look back. He kept a hold of the orange sled. Branches grabbed at him. Twigs slapped him in the face. He tried to keep quiet, but the snaps and cracks were explosions he couldn't prevent. He couldn't see his feet in the black. Even the sky had disappeared.

He stopped to catch his breath, leaned against a tree and realized in his rush to break out through the window he hadn't put on his coat. He couldn't breathe. His teeth chattered.

"Stop crying," he scolded himself. Han Solo never cried.

The sounds from behind were getting closer. Could he hide, hope the stranger would pass right by? No, the stranger would surely hear the massive pounding of his heart.

He ran recklessly, tripping over stumps and smashing through the thicket. A twig swiped at his cheek and ripped at his ear. Then suddenly he felt the ground slip out from under him. A steep decline forced him to grab onto a branch, to keep from sliding down. Below, he saw the glitter of water. He'd never make it. The woods were too thick, the ridge too steep. The noises were even closer now.

He noticed a clearing to his right. He climbed over the rocks that blocked his path. It wasn't much of a clearing. It looked like an old horse trail, a path worn into the woods but now overgrown. As far as Timmy could see, the path went all the way down to the river, with a few sharp turns. It looked like something from one of his video games, narrow and dangerous and clogged with heaps of snow. It was perfect. Of course, it was also reckless and crazy. His mom would have a fit.

A crack close behind made him jump. He crouched in the snow. Even in the dark he saw the shadow crawling toward him. It looked like a giant insect, tentacles outstretched gripping roots and rocks.

Timmy laid his orange sled in the snow. He crawled in carefully, its angle steep—really steep. He allowed himself one more glance over his shoulder. The shadow edged closer. Timmy pointed the sled into the horse trail. One quick shove, and the sled plunged downward.

Nick stood at the edge of the woods, every nerve ending on alert. It was impossible to see with only a flashlight. The black figure was gone. Or hiding.

He remembered a road that snaked through the woods, not far from here. It went all the way to the river. He'd have a better chance with the Jeep. He hurried back toward the church. When he stuffed his gun into the shoulder holster, he realized the other bulge in his jacket was Christine's cellular phone.

Lucy answered on the second ring.

"Lucy, it's Nick."

"Nick, where in the world are you?"

"I don't have time to explain. I'm going to need some men and searchlights. I think I just chased the killer into the woods, behind the old church. He's probably headed for the river again."

"Where do you want the guys to meet you?"

When he had given her the directions, he slapped the phone shut, and returned to the church. He stopped at the window, kicked aside the wood and glass, then crouched to shine light through the hole. Sure enough, there was a bed, posters on the wall, a crate with food. Someone had been staying here. The light reflected off a glimpse of chain. Or someone had been imprisoned here. He saw the comic books, the scattered baseball cards and the small child's coat. Timmy's coat. Then he saw the bloody pillow.

Maggie counted eleven steps, carrying her deep into the ground where the damp air became heavier with each step. The space in which she found herself resembled an old storm cellar. Other than a solid wooden shelf-unit and a large crate in the corner, it was empty. Even the shelves were empty, coated with cobwebs and rat feces. Disappointingly, there were no signs of Timmy and no tunnel.

Still, someone had cleared the snow from the door and attempted to hide it with the tarp. Was there something here, a clue, anything to help find Timmy? On closer inspection, the old wooden crate was actually in good shape with no signs of decay. It certainly had not spent much time in the wet dark hole. Very little dirt covered its surface. Even the lid was attached with shiny new nails.

Maggie holstered her revolver. She found a broken steel rod in a corner and began using it to prise up the lid. The nails screeched but held. Immediately, a rancid smell leaked out, quickly filling the small space. Maggie stopped and backed off just a few steps to examine the crate again. Was it big enough to hide a body? A child's body? She prised at the lid again. This time the smell made her gag. She spat out the penlight she had anchored between her teeth and let it lie on the ground. She held her breath and tried again.

Something scraped in the dirt. Maggie spun around. In the black there was movement. Something bigger than a rat. She dropped to her knees, grabbing for the penlight. She clutched the steel rod, holding it above her head, ready to strike. Then she held her breath again and listened. All sound, all movement had come to a halt. She switched on the penlight. The narrow beam whipped across the opposite wall. The wooden shelves leaned forward, having been shoved away from the wall. Maggie now saw a hole, large enough to be an entrance to the famed tunnel.

In the silence, something stirred behind her. And just as her fingers snuck inside her jacket in search of her gun, a smooth knife blade slid under her chin.

"Agent Maggie O'Dell, what a lovely surprise!"

Maggie didn't recognize the muffled voice in her ear. The knife's razor-sharp point pressed into the softness of her neck. It pushed with a steady pressure, forcing her head back until her neck lay completely exposed, completely vulnerable. She felt a trickle of blood run down inside the collar of her jacket.

"Why a surprise? I thought you'd be expecting me. You seem to know so much about me." With every syllable she felt the knife dig deeper.

"Drop the steel rod." He pulled her against him, wrapping his free arm around the front of her, squeezing harder than necessary to emphasize his strength.

She dropped the rod while he dug inside her jacket. He carefully grabbed the butt of the gun. He tossed it into a dark corner where she heard it knock against the crate. She wasn't surprised that he was much more comfortable using the knife.

She tried to concentrate on his voice and the feel of him. He was strong and four to six inches taller than her. The rest of himself, he disguised. A brush of rubber against her ear and the muffled sound told her he wore a mask. Even his hands were camouflaged in gloves.

"I wasn't expecting you. I thought perhaps you might have gone back home to your safe condo and your lawyer husband and your sick mother. How is your mother, by the way?"

"Why don't you tell me?"

The blade pushed up. Another trickle of blood found its way down her neck, traveling between her breasts.

"That wasn't very nice," he scolded.

"Sorry," she said carefully. She could play his game. She needed to stay calm, level the playing field somehow. "The smell is getting to me. Maybe we could discuss this outside."

"No, sorry. I'm afraid you won't be leaving here at all. What do you think of your new home?" He made her turn around to examine the area with her penlight while the knife scraped her flesh. "Or should I say your tomb?"

"It won't matter…getting rid of me." She talked slowly. "The entire sheriff's department knows who you are. About a dozen deputies will be here in a few minutes."

"Now, Agent O'Dell, you can't bluff me. I know you like to be on your own. That's what got you in trouble with Mr. Stucky, isn't it? And all you have on me is your little psychological profile. I bet I even know what it says. My mother abused me as a child, right? She turned me into a fag, so I murder little boys now."

"Actually, I don't think your mother abused you." She tried frantically to remember what little family history she had found on Father Keller. Of course, his mother had been a single parent just like the victims' mothers. But she had died when Keller was young—a fatal accident.

"I think she loved you," Maggie continued. "And you loved her. But you *were* abused." A twitch told her she was right. "By a relative…perhaps a friend of your mother's…no, a stepfather," she remembered suddenly.

The knife slipped, only a quarter of an inch, but she could breathe again. He was quiet, waiting, listening. She had his attention. It was her move.

"You don't kill little boys for kicks. You try to save them because they remind you of that scared, vulnerable little boy from your past. They remind you of yourself. Do you think that by saving them, you might be able to save yourself?"

His silence continued.

"You deliver these poor boys from evil, is that it? By inflicting your own evil, you transform them into martyrs. You're quite a hero. You might even say yours is a perfect evil."

His arm squeezed tight and jerked her back against him. She had gone too far. The knife shot up to her throat, this time lengthwise so that the sharp blade pressed full against her skin. In one quick motion, he could slit her throat.

"That's psychological bullshit. You don't know what you're talking about." The low guttural sound came from someplace deep inside him. "Albert Stucky should have gutted you when he had a chance. Now, I guess, I'll have to finish the job. We need more light." He dragged her to the tunnel's entrance and extracted a lantern. "Light it." He shoved her to her knees, keeping the knife at her throat and throwing a matchbook into the dirt. "Light it so that you can watch."

"I want you to watch," she heard Albert Stucky say, as if he stood in the dark corner, waiting. "I want you to see how I do it."

She lit the lantern. The yellow glow filled the small space. Her entire body felt numb. She recognized all the familiar signs. It was Albert Stucky all over again. Her body responded to the overwhelming terror by simply shutting down.

The knife blade continued to press against her throat. There was a slight tremble in his hand. Was it from anger or fear? Did it matter?

"Why aren't you crying or screaming?" It was anger.

She didn't answer, couldn't answer. Even her voice had abandoned her. He grabbed her by the hair and yanked her back to her feet, the knife a permanent fixture at her throat.

"Say something!" he screamed at the back of her head. "Plead with me. Pray."

"Just do it," Maggie said quietly, having to coax her voice, her lips, her bruised and cut throat to cooperate just for those three simple words.

"What?"

"Just do it."

"Maggie?" Nick's voice from the top of the stairs.

The stranger spun around, startled and swinging Maggie along with him. As if watching from the corner, she saw her hand grab at the knife, grabbing his wrist. She twisted out from his grasp just as he jerked his hand away and slashed at her, the metal disappearing into her jacket, ripping fabric and flesh. He shoved her away, sending her into the dirt wall with a loud thump.

Nick's stream of light came racing down the steps just as the black shadow grabbed the lantern and plunged into the hole. The wooden shelves teetered, then crashed to the floor, almost hitting Nick.

"Maggie?"

"In the tunnel." She pointed while struggling to her knees. "Don't let him get away."

The tunnel had started to curve and narrow, forcing Nick to crawl on his hands and knees. He could no longer see the masked shadow in front of him. His flashlight revealed only more darkness ahead. Broken roots snaked out of the earth, sometimes dangling in front of him, sticking to his face like cobwebs.

Fur brushed against his hand. He flung the flashlight, missing the rat and sending the batteries flying. The sudden darkness surprised him. Terror exploded inside him. Frantically he groped for the flashlight. One battery, two, finally three. Please let it work.

He screwed the flashlight together. Nothing. He slapped it, tightened the clasp, slapped it again. Light, thank God! He crawled faster. The tunnel narrowed even more.

How could the shadow have disappeared so quickly? And if this was the killer, who had Nick seen disappear into the woods earlier?

How much farther? Was it a trap? Had he missed a turn somewhere back in the beginning where the tunnel seemed huge? Where he had walked crouched low, but still upright? Could he have missed another secret passage? That would explain why he couldn't see or hear the stranger up ahead. What if this tunnel led to a dead end, a wall of dirt?

Just as he felt certain he could go no farther, the flashlight caught a sliver of glittering white up ahead. Snow—it clogged the tunnel. In one last mad rush of panic, Nick clawed, pushed, tore and dug his way to the surface. Suddenly, he saw the black, starlit sky. And despite the miles he thought he had traveled, he realized he hadn't even left the cemetery. He rose from the ground like a corpse among the tombstones. Less than three feet away, the black angel hovered above him with a ghostly radiance that looked like a smile.

Christine's neck ached as it usually did when she fell asleep on the sofa. She saw branches sticking through glass. Had the storm sent branches through her living-room window? She had heard a crash. And there was a hole in the ceiling. Yes, she could even see stars, thousands of them right there, sitting on top of her house.

Where was Grandma Morrelli's afghan? She needed something to stop the draft, to prevent the cold from swirling up around her. If only she could push the furniture off her chest. And where were her arms when she needed them?

Those annoying headlights made her eyes sting. If she could just find the plug, she could shut them off. They made the branches dance, a slow-motion rumba, bumping and grinding glass. It was too hard to keep her eyes open, anyway. Perhaps she could fall back to sleep if only that rasping sound would stop. It came from somewhere inside her coat, from somewhere inside her chest. Whatever it was, it was annoying and…and painful…yes, it was annoyingly painful.

What was President Nixon doing in the headlights? He waved at her. She tried to wave back, but her arm was still asleep. He came into her living room. He moved all the furniture off her chest. Then President Nixon carried her back to sleep.

Timmy watched his sled drift downstream. The bright orange looked fluorescent in the moonlight. He crouched in the snow, hidden by the cattails along the riverbank. All that catapulting practice on Cutty's Hill had paid off.

He only now realized he had lost a shoe in the jump. His ankle hurt. It looked funny, puffed up, almost twice the size of his other one. Then he looked back and saw a black shadow, spiderwebbing its way down the ridge toward him, and moving quickly.

Timmy glanced back at the sled, now regretting that he hadn't stayed in it. The dark figure came to the bottom of the ridge. He was watching the sled, too. It had drifted too far away for him to see inside. But maybe he believed Timmy had stayed inside. He certainly didn't look as if he was in a rush anymore. In fact, he just stood there, staring at the river.

Out here in the open the stranger looked smaller, and, although it was too dark to see his face, Timmy could tell he wasn't wearing the dead president's mask anymore.

Timmy burrowed down farther into the snow. His teeth started chattering. He hugged his knees to his chest and watched and waited. As soon as the stranger disappeared, Timmy decided he would follow the old road. It looked all uphill from here, but it would be better than the woods again. Besides, it had to lead somewhere.

Finally the stranger fumbled through his pockets, found what he was looking for and lit a cigarette. Then he started walking directly toward Timmy.

Maggie clawed her way up the steps, annoyed that her knees wouldn't support her. Her side burned, a fire blazing deeper and deeper, igniting her stomach and lungs. God, she should be getting good at this by now. Practice made perfect. Yet when she struggled up into the moonlight, the sight of her own blood made her light-headed and nauseated. It covered her side and soaked into her clothes.

She eased out of her jacket, then ripped at the lining until she had a piece big enough to plug up her side. She wrapped chunks of snow inside the fabric, then applied it to the wound. Suddenly, the stars in the sky multiplied. She squeezed her eyes shut against the pain. When she opened them, a figure approached, staggering between the headstones like a drunkard. She reached for her gun, her fingers lingering at the empty holster. Of course, she remembered. Her gun lay somewhere below.

"Maggie?" She recognized Nick's voice. He was covered in mud and dirt, but she welcomed the feel of his arm around her.

"Jesus, Maggie, are you okay?"

"Just a flesh wound. Did you get him?"

"I think there must be a maze of tunnels down there, and I took the wrong one."

"He's probably at the church. Maybe that's where he has Timmy."

"Had."

"What?"

"I found the room where he kept them. Timmy's coat was left

behind. I think we're too late, Maggie. I also saw…there was a bloody pillow."

She leaned her head against his chest.

"Jesus, Maggie. You're bleeding awfully bad. I need to get you to the hospital. I sure as hell am not going to lose two people I love in the same night."

As she clung to his arm she wondered if she had heard him correctly. Did he really just say that he loved her?

They were almost to the Jeep when she remembered the crate. "Nick, wait. We have to go back."

Christine stared up at the stars. On the soft bed of snow and under the wonderfully warm and scratchy wool blanket, she hardly noticed that she was lying on the side of the road. And if only she could breathe without choking up chunks of blood, maybe she could sleep. Reality came in short bursts of pain and memories. Eddie fondling her breast. Smashed metal against her legs, crushing her chest. And Timmy, oh, God, Timmy. She tried to sit up, but her body refused to listen, couldn't comprehend the commands. It hurt to breathe. Couldn't she just stop breathing, at least for a few minutes?

The headlights came out of nowhere, rounding the corner and barreling down on her. She heard the brakes screech. Gravel pelted metal. Tires skidded. The light blinded her. When two stretched shadows emerged from the vehicle, she imagined aliens with bulbous heads and bulging insect eyes. Then she realized it was the hats that made their heads look oversize.

"Christine. Oh, my good Lord, it's Christine."

She smiled and closed her eyes. She had never heard that kind of fear and panic in her father's voice. How totally inappropriate for her to be pleased by it.

When her father and Lloyd Benjamin knelt beside her, the only thing she could think to say was, "Eddie knows where Timmy is."

Nick tried to convince Maggie to stay in the Jeep. They had stopped the bleeding for now, but there was no telling how much blood she had already lost.

"You don't understand, Nick," she continued to argue with him.

"I'll go check what's in the stupid crate," he said. "You wait here."

"It may be Timmy."

"What?"

"Inside the crate."

The realization struck him like a fist.

"Why would he do that?"

"Whatever is in the crate might be for my benefit."

"I don't understand."

"Remember the last note? If he knows about Stucky, he may have resorted to Stucky's habits. Nick, it could be Timmy inside that crate. And if it is, it isn't something you should see."

He stared at her. Blood and dirt streaked her face. More dirt and cobwebs filled her hair. Those beautiful full lips held tight against the pain. Those soft, smooth shoulders slouched from the effort to hold herself up. And still she wanted to protect him.

He turned on his heels and stomped back up the hill.

"Nick, wait."

He ignored her calls.

He hesitated at the steps. Then forced himself back down into the earth. The entire space reeked with the stifling smell. He found a steel rod and Maggie's revolver, which he slid into his jacket pocket. Then he tucked the rod and flashlight under his arm and hoisted the crate, lugging it slowly up the steps until he was out of the hellhole, until he could breathe fresh air again.

Maggie was there, leaning against a headstone.

"Let me," she insisted, reaching for the rod.

"I can do this, Maggie." He shoved the rod under the lid and started pumping up and down. The nails screeched and echoed in the silent darkness. Even with the breeze and in the cold the smell of death overpowered the senses. Once the lid snapped free, he hesitated again. Maggie came to his side, reached around him and pulled open the lid.

Tucked carefully inside and wrapped in a white cloth was the small, delicate body of Matthew Tanner.

There was no place for Timmy to run. Nowhere to hide. He slipped down the riverbank, close to the water.

The stranger had stopped just above him. In the silence, Timmy heard him mumbling to himself, but he couldn't make out the words. He'd have to make a run for it, back into the woods. At least there he could hide. He'd never make it in the water. His shivers from the cold were already close to convulsions. The water would only make it worse.

Timmy peeked over the riverbank. The stranger was lighting another cigarette. Now. He needed to go now. He scrambled up the bank, kicking rocks and dirt into the water. He barely made it to the road before his ankle buckled under him. He slammed down on knees and elbows. He struggled to his feet, then suddenly flew up off the ground. He kicked at air and clawed at the arm around his waist. Another arm squeezed his neck.

"Settle down, you little shit."

Timmy started screaming and shouting. The arm squeezed harder, cutting off his air, choking him.

When the car came squealing down the winding road, the stranger still kept his viselike grip on Timmy. The car skidded to a stop in front of them, and still the stranger made no attempt to move or flee. The headlights blinded Timmy, but he recognized Deputy Hal in the driving seat. Why didn't the stranger release him? Timmy's neck hurt bad. He clawed at the arm again. Why didn't the stranger make a run for it?

"What's going on here?" Deputy Hal demanded. He and another deputy got out of the car and approached slowly.

Couldn't they tell what was going on? Couldn't they tell the stranger was hurting him?

"I found the kid hiding in the woods," the stranger told them, only he sounded excited and proud. "You might say I rescued him."

"I see that," said Deputy Hal.

No, it was a lie. Timmy wanted to tell them it was all a lie, but he couldn't breathe, couldn't speak with the arm squeezing his neck. Why were they looking as if they believed the stranger? He was the killer. Couldn't they see that?

"Why don't the two of you get in with us? Come on, Timmy. You're safe now."

Slowly the arm released Timmy's neck. His feet touched the ground. Timmy pulled free and ran to Deputy Hal, tripping on his swollen ankle.

Hal grabbed Timmy by the shoulders and gently shoved him behind him. Then Deputy Hal pulled out his gun and said to the stranger, "Come on, now. You've got a lot of explaining to do, Eddie."

87

Friday, October 31

Christine awoke to a room full of flowers. Had she died, after all? Through a blur, she saw her mother sitting next to the bed, and knew immediately that she was, in fact, still alive. Certainly the blue and pink jogging suit her mother wore would never be acceptable attire for heaven—or hell.

"How are you feeling?" Her mother smiled and reached for Christine's hand.

Her mother was finally letting her hair go gray. It looked good. Christine decided to tell her later when a compliment would come in handy to combat the inquisition.

"Where am I?"

"In the hospital, dear. Don't you remember? You just got out of surgery a little while ago."

Surgery? Only now did Christine notice all the tubes going in and out of her. In a moment of panic, she ripped off the covers.

"Christine!"

Her legs were still there. Thank God. She could move them. There were bandages on one, but she didn't care as long as the leg moved.

"You don't need to catch pneumonia." Her mother tucked the covers back in around her.

Christine raised both arms, flexed the fingers and watched the fluids drip into her veins. The pieces all seemed there and working. That her chest and stomach felt like chunks of beaten and sliced chopped liver didn't matter. At least she was all in one piece.

"Your father and Bruce went for coffee. They'll be so pleased to find you awake."

"Bruce is here?" Then Christine remembered Timmy, and the panic began to suck all the air from the room.

"Give him a second chance, Christine. This ordeal has really changed him."

Just then, Nick peeked into the room. There was a new cut on his forehead, but the bruises and swelling around his jaw were hardly noticeable. He was dressed in a crisp blue shirt, navy tie, blue jeans and navy sports jacket. He looked dressed for a funeral. She remembered Timmy again. A new wave of terror came crashing down on her.

"Hi, honey," their mother said as Nick leaned down to kiss her cheek.

Christine studied the two of them, watching for signs. Did she dare ask? Would they only lie to protect her? Did they think she was too fragile?

"I want the truth, Nicky," she blurted out in a voice so shrill she hardly recognized it as her own. She could see in Nick's eyes that he knew exactly what she was talking about.

"Okay. If that's the way you want it." He headed back for the door, and opened it. Timmy stood there. Christine rubbed her eyes. Was she hallucinating again? Timmy hobbled toward her, and she could see the scratches and bruises, a cut on one cheek and a purple swollen lip. However, his face and hair were scrubbed clean, his clothes crisp and fresh. He even wore new tennis shoes.

"Hi, Mom," he said as though it were any other morning. He crawled into the chair his grandmother held out for him, kneeling and making himself tall enough to look over the bed. She allowed the tears, had no choice, really. Was he real? She touched his shoulder, smoothed down his cowlick and caressed his cheek.

"Aw, Mom. Everybody's watching," he said, and she knew he was real.

Nick escaped before it got mushy. He turned the corner and almost ran into his father, who stepped back, as though worried the coffee he carried would spill.

"Careful there, son. You're gonna miss quite a bit being in such a hurry."

Nick checked his father's eyes and immediately saw the sarcastic criticism. He was in too good a mood to let his father spoil it. So he smiled and started to walk around him.

"It's not Eddie, you know," his father called after him.

"Yeah?" Nick stopped and turned. "Well, this time that'll be up to a court of law to decide and not Antonio Morrelli."

"What the hell is that supposed to mean?"

Nick took a step closer until he was standing eye to eye with his father.

"Did you help plant evidence against Jeffreys?"

"Watch your mouth, boy. I never planted a thing."

"Then how did you explain the discrepancies?"

"As far as I was concerned, there were no discrepancies. I did what was necessary to convict that son of a bitch."

"You ignored evidence."

"I knew Jeffreys killed that little Wilson boy. You didn't *see* that boy. You didn't see what he made that boy go through. Jeffreys deserved to die."

"I've seen enough this week to last me a lifetime," Nick replied. "Maybe Jeffreys did deserve to die. But by pinning the other two murders on him, you let another murderer get away. You closed the investigation. You made a community feel safe again."

"I did what I thought was necessary."

"Don't tell me. Tell that to Laura Alverez and Michelle Tanner. Tell them how you did what was necessary."

Nick walked away. There was little victory in telling Antonio Morrelli he had been wrong. But as his boot heels echoed down the quiet hall, he walked a bit taller.

He stopped by the nurses' station and was startled by the unit secretary dressed in a black cape and witch's hat. It took a minute before he noticed the orange and black crepe paper and pumpkin cutouts. Of course, today was Halloween.

"Hi, Nick," she said. "What can we do for you?"

"Can you tell me Agent O'Dell's room number?"

"It's 372. At the end of the hall and to the right. Although she may be gone."

"Gone?"

"She checked out earlier and was just waiting for some clothes. Hers were pretty trashed when she came in last night," she explained, but Nick already was halfway down the hall.

He burst through the door without knocking, startling Maggie, who turned quickly from the window, then positioned her back—and the open hospital gown—to the wall.

"Jesus, Morrelli, don't you knock?"

"Sorry."

She looked wonderful. The short, dark hair was smooth and shiny again. Her creamy skin had some color. And her eyes actually sparkled.

"They said you might be gone."

"I'm waiting for some clothes. One of the hospital volunteers offered to go shopping for me." She paced, carefully using the wall to shield her back. "That was about two hours ago. I just hope she doesn't come back with something pink."

"The doctor said it's okay for you to check out?"

"He's leaving it to my discretion."

She caught him staring at her, and when their eyes met, he held her gaze. He didn't care if she saw the concern. In fact, he wanted her to see it.

"How's Christine?" she asked.

"Surgery went well."

"What about her leg?"

"There won't be any permanent damage. I just took Timmy in to see her."

"If I didn't know better, I'd almost believe in happy endings," she said.

Her eyes met his again, this time accompanied by a faint smile, a slight tug at the corners of her lips. Jesus, she was beautiful when she smiled. He wanted to tell her that. Opened his mouth, in fact, to do just that, then thought better of it. Did she have any idea how scared he was when he thought she'd left without so much as a goodbye? Could she even tell what effect she had on him? The hell with her husband, her marriage. He needed to take the risk, let the chips fall where they may. He needed to tell her he loved her.

Instead, he said, "We arrested Eddie Gillick this morning."

She sat on the edge of the bed and waited for more.

"We brought in Ray Howard again for questioning. This time he admitted that sometimes he loaned the old blue pickup to Eddie."

"The day Danny disappeared?"

"Howard conveniently couldn't remember. But there's more—lots more. Eddie came to work for the sheriff's department the summer before the first killings. The Omaha Police Department had given him a letter of recommendation, but there were three separate reprimands in his file, all for unnecessary force while making arrests. Two of the cases were juveniles. He even broke one kid's arm."

"What about the last rites?"

"Eddie's mom—a single mom, by the way—worked two jobs just to send him to Catholic school, all the way through high school."

"I don't know, Nick."

She didn't look convinced. It didn't surprise him. He went on with the rest.

"He would have had access to the evidence in Jeffreys' case and could easily have framed him. He's also had access to the morgue. In fact, he was there yesterday afternoon picking up the autopsy photos. He could easily have snatched Matthew's body when he realized the teeth marks in the photos might ID him. Plus, it would have been easy for him to make a few phone calls, use his badge number and get information on Albert Stucky."

"The morgue is never locked," Maggie countered. "Anyone could have had access. And much of what happened with Stucky was publicized in the tabloids."

"There's still more." He'd left this for last. The most incriminating evidence was the most questionable. "We found some stuff in the trunk of his car." He let her see his skepticism. Was it Ronald Jeffreys all over again? They were both thinking the same thing.

"What kind of stuff?"

"The Halloween mask, a pair of black gloves and some rope."

"Why would he have all that in the trunk of his abandoned car if he knew we were hot on his trail? Especially if he was responsible for framing Jeffreys in the same manner? Also, how did he have time to do all this?"

It was exactly what Nick had wondered, but he wanted desperately for this to be all over.

"My dad just more or less admitted that he knew someone may have planted evidence."

"He admitted that?"

"Let's just say he admitted to ignoring the discrepancies."

"Does your father think Eddie could be the killer?"

"He said he's sure it's not Eddie."

"And that makes you even more convinced that it is?" Jesus, she knew him well.

"Timmy has a lighter the guy gave him. It has the sheriff's department emblem on it. It's a reward type thing that my dad used. He never handed out that many of them. Eddie was one of about five."

"Lighters get lost," she said. She stood up and slowly made her way to the window.

This time her mind was clearly far away. She even forgot about the slit in the back of her hospital gown. Though from this angle he could only see a sliver of her back, part of her shoulder. The gown made her look small and vulnerable. He imagined wrapping his arms around her, wrapping his entire body around hers. He simply wanted to get lost in her for a very long time.

"You still think it's Keller?" he asked, but knew the answer.

"I don't know. Maybe it's just hard for me to realize I'm losing my touch."

Nick could certainly relate to that.

"Eddie doesn't fit your profile?"

"The man in that cellar wasn't some hothead who lost his temper and sliced up little boys. This was a mission for him, a well-thought-out and planned mission. Somehow, I really do think he believes he's saving these boys."

She stared out of the window. "What does Timmy say?" she asked. "Can he identify Eddie as the man who held him prisoner?"

"He seemed certain last night, but that was after Eddie chased him down the ridge and grabbed him. Eddie claims he spotted Timmy in the woods and went after him to rescue him. This morning Timmy admitted he never saw the man's face. But, it can't all be just coincidence, can it?"

"No, it does sound like you have a case." She shrugged.

"But do I have a killer?"

He stuffed his few belongings into the old suitcase. It was the only thing he had of his mother's.

He had stolen it out from under his stepfather's bed the night he ran away from home. Home—that was certainly a misnomer. It had never felt like his home, even less after his mother was gone. Without her, the two-story brick house had become a prison, and he had taken his punishment nightly for almost three weeks before he left.

Even the night of his escape, he had waited until after his stepfather had finished and then collapsed from exhaustion. He had stolen his mother's suitcase and packed while blood trickled down the insides of his legs. Unlike his mother, he had refused to grow accustomed to his stepfather's deep, violent thrusts, the fresh tears and old ones not allowed to heal. That night, he had barely been able to walk, but still he had managed somehow to make it the six miles to Our Lady of Lourdes Catholic Church where Father Daniel had offered refuge.

A similar price had been paid for his room and board, but at least Father Daniel had been kind and gentle and small. There had been no more rips and tears, only the humiliation, which he had accepted as part of his punishment. He was, after all, a murderer. That horrible look still haunted his sleep. That look of utter surprise in his mother's dead eyes as she lay sprawled on the basement floor, her body twisted and broken.

He slammed the suitcase shut, hoping to slam out the image.

His second murder had been much easier, a stray tomcat Father Daniel had taken in. Unlike himself, the cat had received room and board with no price to pay. Perhaps that alone had been reason enough to kill it. He remembered its warm blood had splattered his hands and face when he slashed its throat.

From then on, each murder had become a spiritual revelation, a sacrificial slaughter. It wasn't until his second year of seminary that he murdered his first boy, an unsuspecting delivery boy with sad eyes and freckles. The boy had reminded him of himself. So, of course, he needed to kill him, to get the boy out of his misery, to save him, to save himself.

He checked his watch and knew he had plenty of time. He carefully placed the old suitcase by the door, next to the gray and black duffel bag he had packed earlier. Then he glanced at the newspaper folded neatly on his bed, the headline garnering yet another smile: SHERIFF'S DEPUTY SUSPECTED IN BOYS' MURDERS.

How wonderfully easy it had been. He knew the minute he had found Eddie Gillick's lighter on the floor of the old blue pickup that the slick and arrogant bully would make the perfect patsy. Almost as perfect as Jeffreys had been.

All those evenings of excruciating small talk, playing cards with the egomaniac, had finally paid off. He had pretended to be interested in Gillick's latest sexual conquest, only to offer forgiveness and absolution when the good deputy finally sobered up. He had pretended to be Gillick's friend when, in fact, the conceited know-it-all turned his stomach. Gillick's bragging had also revealed a short temper, mostly targeted at "punk kids" and "cock-teasing sluts" who, according to Gillick, "had it coming". In many ways, Eddie Gillick reminded him of his stepfather, which would make Gillick's conviction even sweeter.

And why wouldn't Gillick be convicted, with his self-destructive behavior and all that damning evidence tucked neatly inside the trunk of the deputy's very own smashed Chevy? What luck, stumbling across it in the woods like that, making it so easy to stash the fatal evidence. Just like Jeffreys.

He remembered how Ronald Jeffreys had come to him, confessing to Bobby Wilson's murder. When Jeffreys asked for forgiveness there hadn't been a shred of remorse in his voice. Jeffreys deserved what had happened to him. And it had been so simple, too. One anonymous phone call to the sheriff's department and some incriminating evidence was all it had taken.

Yes, Ronald Jeffreys had been the perfect patsy just like Daryl Clemmons. The young seminarian had shared his homosexual fears with him, unknowingly setting himself up for the murder of that poor, defenseless paperboy. That poor boy whose body was found near the river that ran along the seminary.

Then there was Randy Maiser, an unfortunate transient, who had come to St Mary's Catholic Church seeking refuge. The people of Wood River had been quick to convict the ragged stranger when one of their little boys ended up dead.

Ronald Jeffreys, Daryl Clemmons and Randy Maiser—all of them such perfect patsies. And now, Eddie Gillick could be added to that list.

He glanced at the newspaper again, and his eyes rested on Timmy's photo. Disappointment clouded his good mood. Though Timmy's escape had brought a surprising amount of relief, it was that very escape that required his own sudden exodus. How could he continue his day-to-day routine knowing he had failed the boy? And, eventually, Timmy would recognize his eyes, his walk, his guilt. Guilt because he hadn't been able to save Timmy Hamilton. Unless…

He grabbed the newspaper and flipped to the inside story of Timmy's escape and his mother, Christine's, accident. He scanned the article using his index finger until he noticed the ragged fingernail, bitten to the quick. He tucked his fingers into a fist, ashamed of their appearance. Then he found the paragraph, almost at the end. Yes, Timmy's estranged father, Bruce, was back in town.

He glanced at his watch again. Poor Timmy. Perhaps somehow, someway, Timmy deserved a second chance at salvation. Surely he could make time for something that important.

Maggie wanted to tell Nick it was over. That no more little boys would disappear. But even as they went over the case against Eddie Gillick, she couldn't dislodge that gnawing doubt.

She wished the hospital volunteer would be as punctual as she had been perky. How could anyone carry on a serious conversation in these paper-thin gowns? And would it be so much trouble to provide a robe, a sash, anything to prevent a full view of her unprotected backside?

She could see Nick's eyes exercising extreme caution, but all it took was a few unintentional slips to remind her of how naked she was under the loose garment. Worse yet was that damn tingle that spread over her skin every time his eyes were on her. And that stupid fluttering sensation that teased between her thighs. It was like radar. Her entire body reacted beyond her control to its own nakedness and Nick's presence.

"Okay, so it does look as though Eddie Gillick could be guilty," she admitted, "but what was Christine doing with Eddie last night?"

"I haven't talked to her about it this morning. Last night she said Eddie was supposed to take her home, but he took a detour. He told her if she had sex with him, he'd tell her where Timmy was."

"He said he knew where Timmy was?"

"That's what Christine said. Of course, I think she was delusional. She also told me President Nixon carried her to the side of the road."

"The mask, of course. He carried Christine out of the car then stuffed his disguise into the trunk."

"Then hurried along to chase Timmy through the woods," Nick added. "This, of course, is after he tried to rape Christine, then attack you in the graveyard cellar. Busy guy."

"Ms. O'Dell?" A nurse peeked around the door. "You have a visitor."

"It's about time," Maggie said, expecting the hospital volunteer with her clothes.

The nurse held open the door and smiled at the handsome, golden-haired man in the black Armani suit. He carried an overnight case, and a matching garment bag was slung over his arm.

"Hi, Maggie."

"Greg? What in the world are you doing here?"

Timmy listened for the vending machine to swallow his quarters before he made his selection. He almost chose a Snickers, but his gut remembered, and he punched the Reese's button, instead.

He tried not to think about the stranger or the little room. He needed to stay focused on his mom and help her get better. It scared him to see her in that huge white hospital bed, hooked up to all those machines that gurgled, wheezed and clicked. She seemed to be okay, even seemed happy to see his dad after, of course, she had yelled at him. But this time his dad didn't yell back. He just kept saying he was sorry. When Timmy left the room, his dad was holding his mom's hand, and she actually let him. That had to be a good sign, didn't it?

Timmy sat in the plastic waiting-room chair. He unwrapped his candy bar and separated out the two pieces. He popped one whole peanut butter cup into his mouth and let it melt before he started chewing.

"I thought you were a Snickers guy."

Timmy spun around in the chair. He hadn't even heard footsteps.

"Hi, Father Keller," he mumbled over a mouthful.

"How are you, Timmy?" The priest patted Timmy's shoulder, his hand lingering on Timmy's back.

"I'm okay." He swallowed the rest of the candy bar, clearing his mouth. "My mom had surgery this morning."

"I heard." Father Keller slid a duffel bag into the seat next to Timmy's, then knelt down in front of him.

Timmy liked that about Father Keller, how he made him feel special. He was genuinely interested. Timmy could see that in his eyes, those soft blue eyes. Those eyes… Timmy looked again and suddenly a knot twisted in his stomach. Today, there was something different about Father Keller's eyes.

"You going someplace?" Timmy asked, swinging a thumb at the duffel bag.

"I'm taking Father Francis to his burial place. In fact, that's why I'm here, to make sure the body is ready."

"He's here?"

"Down in the morgue. Would you like to come with me?"

"I don't know. I'm waiting for my grandpa."

"It'll only take a few minutes, and I think you'll enjoy seeing it. It looks like something out of *The X-Files*."

"Really?" Timmy remembered watching Special Agent Scully doing autopsies. "You sure it's okay if I come along? Won't the hospital people get mad?"

"Nah, there's never anyone down there."

Father Keller stood up and grabbed the duffel bag. He waited while Timmy shoved the rest of the Reese's into his mouth, accidentally dropping the wrapper. When he knelt to pick it up, Timmy noticed Father Keller's Nikes, crisp and white, as usual. Only today there was…there was a knot in one of the shoestrings. A knot holding it together. The knot in Timmy's stomach tightened.

Why did Father Keller have a knot in his shoestring?

"How did you find out I was in the hospital?" Maggie asked when she and Greg were alone. He had collected her overnight bag at the airport, and brought it back to her. She spread out the suits she had carefully packed days ago, pleased with their appearance despite two trips halfway across the country.

"Actually, I didn't know until I arrived at the sheriff's department earlier this morning. This just reiterates my point, Maggie."

"Your point?"

"That this job is much too dangerous."

"For whom, Greg? You? Because I don't have a problem with it. I've always known there would be risks."

She stayed calm, glanced over her shoulder at him. He was pacing, hands on his hips as if waiting for a verdict.

"When I asked you to pick up my bags from the airport, I didn't mean for you to deliver them." She tried a smile, but he looked determined not to let her off so easily.

"Next year I'll make partner. We're on our way, Maggie."

"On our way to what?" She pulled out a matching bra and panties.

"You shouldn't have to do all this dangerous fieldwork. For God's sake, Maggie, you've got eight stinking years with the Bureau. You finally have the clout to be…I don't know, a supervisor, an instructor."

"I enjoy what I do, Greg." She yanked off the gown and struggled into the panties. It hurt to bend, to lift her arms. She was grateful a bandage covered the unsightly stitches.

"Oh, my God, Maggie."

She spun around to find him staring at her wounded shoulder, a grimace contorting his features. She couldn't help wondering whether it was disgust or concern. His eyes examined the rest of her body, finally resting on the scar below her breasts. Suddenly, she felt exposed and embarrassed, neither of which made sense. He was her husband, after all. Yet she grabbed the gown and pressed it to her breasts.

"Not all of those are from last night," he said. "Why didn't you tell me?"

She threw the gown aside.

"This is from over a month ago, Greg," she said, tracing the scar that Stucky had left. "Most husbands would have noticed. But we don't even have sex anymore, so how could you notice? You haven't even noticed that I don't sleep next to you. That I spend most nights pacing. You don't care about me, Greg."

"This is ridiculous. How can you say I don't care about you? That's exactly why I want you to leave the Bureau."

"If you really cared, you'd understand how important my job is to me. No, you're more concerned about how I make you look. That's why you don't want me in the field. You want to be able to tell your friends and associates that I have some big FBI title. You want me to be able to wear sexy black cocktail dresses to your fancy attorney parties so you can show me off, and my hideous scars don't fit into that scenario. Well, this is me, Greg," she said with her hands on her hips. "This is who I am. Maybe I just don't fit into your country-club lifestyle anymore. Thank you for bringing my things," she added quietly, calmly. "Now, I want you to leave."

"Fine. Why don't we get together for lunch after you've cooled off?"

"No, I want you to go back home."

He stared at her, his gray eyes going cold, his pursed lips stifling angry words. She waited for his next onslaught, but he turned on his expensive leather heels and stomped out.

Maggie collapsed onto the bed, the pain in her side only a minor contributor to her exhaustion. She barely heard the tap on the door but braced herself for the rest of Greg's fury. Instead, Nick came in, took one look at her and spun around.

"Sorry, I didn't realize you weren't dressed."

She jumped up, grabbed the bra and wrestled into it. The wound in her side slowed her down.

"Actually, I should be the one to apologize," she said. "It seems my scarred body repulses men." She snatched a blouse and thrust her arms into it.

Nick glanced over his shoulder. "Jesus, Maggie, you should know by now that I'm the wrong one to say that to. I've been trying for days now to find one little thing about you that doesn't turn me on."

She heard the smile in his voice. Her fingers stopped at the buttons, a slight tremor making it difficult to continue as the heat crawled down her body. She stared at the back of him and wondered how in the world Nick Morrelli could make her feel so sensuous, so alive without even looking at her.

"Anyway, I didn't mean to barge in on you," he said, "but there's a slight problem with bringing in Father Keller for questioning."

"I know, I know. We don't have enough evidence."

"No, that's not it."

"What's the problem?" she asked.

"I just called the rectory and talked to the cook. Father Keller is gone and so is Ray Howard."

As soon as they got off the elevator Timmy noticed the sign that read Restricted Area—Hospital Personnel Only. Father Keller didn't seem to notice. He walked down the hallway without even hesitating.

Timmy tried to keep up, although his ankle still hurt. Father Keller glanced down at him.

"What happened to your leg?"

"I guess I sprained my ankle last night in the woods."

"You've been through quite a lot, huh?" The priest stopped, patted Timmy on the head. "You want to talk about it?"

"No, not really."

Father Keller pushed open a door and flipped a light switch. The huge room grew bright as the lights flickered on, one at a time.

"Wow, this does look like *The X-Files*," Timmy said, running his fingers over the spotless counters, stainless steel just like the table in the center of the room. Then he noticed the drawers, lined up side by side in the opposite wall. "Is that…?" He pointed. "Is that where they keep the dead people?"

"Yes, it is," Father Keller said. He carefully placed the duffel bag on the metal table.

"Is Father Francis in one of the drawers?"

"Yes, unless they have already picked up his body."

"Picked up?"

"The mortuary may have already picked up Father Francis and taken him to the airport."

"The airport?" Timmy was confused.

"Yes, remember I told you I was taking Father Francis to his burial place?"

"Oh, okay."

"I hear your father is back in town," Father Keller said, standing next to the table.

"Yeah, I'm hoping he'll stay."

"Really? You'd like your father to stay?"

"Yeah, I guess I would."

"Wasn't he unkind to you?"

The priest unzipped the duffel bag and was immediately preoccupied by its contents.

"How do you mean?" Timmy asked.

"Didn't he hurt you? Didn't he do unpleasant things to you?"

"My dad was mostly nice to me. Sometimes I guess he yelled."

"What about your bruises?"

"I guess I just bruise easily. Most of 'em are from soccer." Soccer and Chad Calloway.

"Then why did your mom make him go away?" Father Keller's voice was low with a hint of anger while his eyes stayed focused inside the bag.

Timmy didn't want to make him mad. He heard the clink of metal and wondered what kind of tools Father Keller had in the bag.

"I don't know for sure. I think it had something to do with a slutty, big-breasted receptionist," Timmy said, trying to use the exact words he had overheard his mom use.

This time Father Keller did look at him, only the piercing blue eyes sent a shiver through Timmy. Usually, Father Keller's eyes were kind and warm. But now…those eyes…no, it couldn't be. Timmy's stomach churned.

"Timmy, are you okay?" Father Keller asked, and suddenly his cold eyes warmed with concern. "I'm sorry if I upset you. Do you think your mom and dad will get back together? Do you think you can be a real family again?"

"I hope so," he answered. "I miss my dad. We used to go camping sometimes. Just the two of us. He'd let me bait my own hook. We'd talk and stuff. It was pretty cool. Except my dad's an awful cook."

Father Keller smiled at him now as he zipped up the duffel bag.

"Here you two are," Grandpa Morrelli said, swinging open the door. "Nurse Richards thought she saw the elevator come down here. What are you two up to?"

"Father Keller is picking up Father Francis for their trip." Timmy checked the priest's face and was pleased to see the smile still there. Then to his grandpa, he said, "Doesn't this look like something from *The X-Files*?"

Mrs. O'Malley, St Margaret's cook, had told Nick that Father Keller's flight left at two forty-five, and that he was escorting Father Francis' body to its final resting place. When Nick had asked to speak with Ray Howard, she said Ray was gone, too.

"Where is Father Francis being buried?"

"Somewhere in Venezuela."

"Venezuela!"

"Father Francis absolutely loved it there. It was his first assignment out of seminary. A small, poor farming parish. I don't remember the name. Yes, Father Francis always talked about how some day he hoped to return. Too bad it couldn't have been under different circumstances."

"Do you remember what city it was close to?"

"No, I can't say that I do. All those places down there are so hard to remember, hard to pronounce. Father Keller will be back next week. Can't this wait until then?"

"No, I'm afraid it can't. What about the flight number or airline?"

"Oh my, I don't know if he said. Maybe TWA… No, United, I think. It leaves at two forty-five out of Eppley," she added, as if that should be all that was necessary.

Now Nick glanced at his watch. It was almost two-thirty. The Friday crowds had descended upon Eppley Airport. Business men and women hurried to get home. Vacationers moved more slowly. Nick slowed his pace when he noticed the tight, pale look on Maggie's face. Of course she was hurting and, of course, she wouldn't complain.

He and Maggie split up at the ticket counters, flashing credentials and badges to shove their way through the lines and hurry the desk clerks.

The tall woman at the TWA counter refused to be rushed by a county sheriff's badge. "I'm sorry, Sheriff Morrelli. I cannot disclose our passenger list or information about any of our passengers. Please, you're holding up the line."

"Okay, okay. How about flights? Do you have a flight to anywhere in Venezuela, say in…" he glanced at his watch again "…in ten to fifteen minutes?"

She checked her computer screen.

"We have a flight to Miami that connects with an international flight to Caracas."

"Great! What gate?"

"Gate 11, but that flight left at two-fifteen."

"Are you sure?"

"Quite sure."

Nick moved over to stand near where Maggie talked to another ticket agent.

"Thanks, anyway," she told the desk clerk at the United counter, then followed him to a corner out of the traffic.

"TWA has a flight to Miami that connects to one that goes on to Caracas," Nick told her, "but it left about twenty minutes ago."

"Was Keller on board?"

"The desk clerk wouldn't tell me. We may need a court order to find out. What do we do now? If he gets to South America we may never find him. Maggie?"

Was she even listening? Her eyes were focused over his shoulder.

"Maggie?"

"I think I just found Ray Howard," she said.

The large gray and black duffel bag he was carrying looked heavy, making Ray Howard's limp more pronounced. He wore his usual uniform of well-pressed brown trousers, white shirt and tie. A navy blazer replaced the cardigan.

"Maybe he simply brought Father Keller to the airport," Nick said in a low voice, though Howard was clear across the ticket lobby, far from overhearing.

"I don't usually take along luggage when I drop people off at the airport," Maggie said.

"Tell me again why he isn't a suspect?" Nick asked without taking his eyes off Howard.

"The limp. Remember the boys may have been carried into the woods. And Timmy was sure the guy didn't limp."

They watched Howard head for the escalators.

"I don't know, Maggie. That duffel bag sure looks heavy."

"Yes, it does," she said, and hurried toward the escalators with Nick alongside.

Howard hesitated at the down escalator, waiting to get his footing right before stepping on.

"Mr. Howard," Maggie called out.

Howard looked over his shoulder, grabbed the railing and did a double take. This time a flash of panic appeared in his lizard eyes. He jumped onto the escalator and ran down the moving steps, clearing a path with the duffel bag, striking and pushing people out of the way.

"I'll take the stairs." Nick raced for the emergency exit. Maggie followed Howard, ripping her revolver from its holster and holding it nose up.

"FBI!" she yelled, clearing her own path.

Howard's speed surprised her. He weaved through the crowd, zigzagging around luggage gurneys and leaping over an abandoned pet carrier. He shoved travelers aside, knocking down a small, blue-haired lady and smashing through a group of Japanese tourists. He kept looking back.

She was closing in on him, though her own breathing disappointed her. The ragged gasps sounded as if they were coming from a ventilator, surely not her own chest. She ignored the flame in her side, burning her flesh once again.

Howard stopped suddenly, grabbed a luggage cart from a stunned flight attendant and shoved it at Maggie. The suitcases snapped free. One burst open, spewing cosmetics, shoes, clothes across the floor. Maggie lost her balance and fell into the mess, smashing a bottle of liquid makeup with her knee.

Howard headed for the parking garage. He pushed open the door just as Nick grabbed his jacket collar and swung him around. Howard fell to his knees and covered his head with his arms as if expecting a blow. Nick's hands, however, didn't leave his collar.

Maggie struggled to her feet while the flight attendant scrambled for her belongings. Nick's eyes were filled with concern for Maggie, even as his hands clutched Howard's collar, rendering him immobile.

"I'm fine," Maggie said before he asked. But when she replaced her revolver, she felt the sticky wetness through her blouse. Her fingertips were smeared with blood when she brought her hand out from inside her jacket.

"What are you doing here, Ray?" Nick demanded.

"I brought Father Keller. He had a flight to catch. Why were you chasing me? I didn't do nothing wrong."

"Then why did you run?"

"Eddie told me to watch out for you two."

"Eddie did?"

"What's in the duffel bag?" Maggie interrupted the two of them.

"I don't know. Father Keller said he wouldn't be needing it anymore. He asked me to take it back for him."

"You mind if we take a peek?" She prised it out of his hands and swung it up onto a nearby chair.

"You sure it's not your bag?" she said, pulling out the familiar brown cardigan and several well-pressed white shirts. Howard's face registered surprise.

A stack of art books accounted for the bag's weight. Maggie put them aside, more interested in the small, carved box tucked between several pairs of boxer shorts. The carved words on the lid were Latin, but she had no idea what they said. The contents didn't surprise her: a white linen cloth, a small crucifix, two candles and a small container of oil. Then Maggie reached underneath the pile of newspaper clippings to the bottom of the box. She pulled out a small pair of boy's underpants tightly wrapped around a shiny fillet knife.

Sunday, November 2

Maggie punched another code into the computer and waited. She took another bite of her blueberry muffin, homemade, special delivery from where else? Wanda's.

Her bags were packed. She had showered and dressed hours ago, but her flight didn't leave until noon. She rubbed her stiff neck and still couldn't believe she had slept the entire night in the straight-backed chair. Even more surprised that she had slept without visions of Albert Stucky dancing in her head.

She grabbed the huge Sunday edition of the *Omaha Journal*. She was glad to see Christine's byline back on the front page. Even from her hospital bed, Christine continued to crank out articles.

Maggie scanned the article once again. Christine's writing now stuck to the facts, letting quotes from the experts draw the sensational conclusions. She found her own quote and read it for the third time.

> Special Agent Maggie O'Dell, an FBI profiler assigned to the case, said it was "unlikely Gillick and Howard were partners. Serial killers," Agent O'Dell insisted, "are loners." However, the district attorney's office has filed murder charges against both former sheriff's deputy Eddie Gillick, and a church janitor, Raymond Howard, for the deaths of Aaron Harper, Eric Paltrow, Danny Alverez and Matthew Tanner. A separate charge has been entered for the kidnapping of Timmy Hamilton.

There was a tap at the door. When she opened it, Nick stood there smiling at her, the dimples in full force. His blue eyes sparkled at her as if there was a special secret his eyes shared with hers. He wore a red T-shirt and blue jeans, both tight enough to outline his athletic body, teasing her eyes and making her fingers ache to touch him. He came into the room. She caught herself checking out his backside, shook her head and silently chastised herself.

"It must be warm out," she heard herself say.

"It's hard to believe we had snow a few days ago. Nebraska weather." He shrugged. "Here, this is for you." He handed her a gift-wrapped box. "Sort of a thank you, slash, goodbye present."

She took it and slowly unwrapped it. She pulled out the red football jersey with a white number seventeen emblazoned on the back. She couldn't help but smile. "It's perfect."

"I don't expect it to replace the Packers, but I thought you should have a Nebraska Cornhuskers, too."

"Thanks. I love it."

"Seventeen was my number," he added. "Oh, and this is from Timmy."

She took the videotape, and as soon as she saw the cover her smile returned. "*The X-Files*."

"He said that it has one of his favorite episodes—the one with the killer cockroaches, of course."

"I'll be sure to watch it and…and I'll let Timmy know what I think," she said, surprised but pleased by the unfamiliar commitment to stay in touch.

They stood there staring at each other. Maggie didn't want to move, couldn't move. They had spent the last week together, almost around the clock, sharing pizza and brandy, exchanging opinions and views, wrestling madmen and holy men, dousing fears and expectations and grieving for small boys neither of whom they knew. She had allowed Nick Morrelli access to vulnerabilities she had shared with no one else, not even herself. Perhaps that was why she suddenly felt as if a major chunk of herself would be left behind.

"Maggie, I—"

"I'm sorry," she interrupted. "I almost forgot. I'm trying to access some information." She returned to the table in the corner. The computer connection had finally been made, and she punched several more keys.

"You're still looking for him," he said without surprise or irritation, coming up behind her.

"From Caracas, Father Francis' body was shipped by truck to a small community about a hundred miles to the south. Keller's airline ticket has him returning today. I'm trying to find out if he boarded the flight back to Miami or if he headed somewhere else."

Finally, the passenger list for TWA flight 1692 materialized on the screen. Maggie found Reverend Michael Keller's name, and it was on the list even after departure.

"Just because he's on the list doesn't mean he was on the plane."

"I know that."

"So what happens if he doesn't come back?"

"I'll find him," she said simply. "What is that saying? He can run, but he can't hide."

"Even if you find him, we don't have a shred of evidence to implicate him."

"Do you honestly believe Eddie Gillick or Ray Howard killed those boys?"

He hesitated.

"I'm not sure what part, if any, Eddie may have played in the murders. But you know I suspected Howard from the beginning. Come on, Maggie. We found him at the airport with what could be the murder weapon."

She frowned at him and shook her head. "He doesn't fit the profile."

"You know what? I don't want to spend my last hour with you talking about Eddie Gillick or Ray Howard or Father Keller or anything to do with this case."

The look in his eyes made the tremble invade her fingers again, and the flutter raced from her stomach to between her thighs.

He touched her face gently, holding her eyes with an intensity that made her feel as though she were the only woman in the world—at least, for the moment. She could easily have stopped the kiss. But when his lips brushed hers, all her energy focused on keeping her knees from buckling. When she didn't protest, his mouth caught hers in a wet, soft kiss filled with urgency and emotion. Even after his mouth left hers, she kept her eyes closed, trying to steady her breathing.

"I love you, Maggie O'Dell."

Her eyes flew open. His face was still close to hers, his eyes serious. She pulled away.

"Nick, we barely know each other."

"I've never felt this way before, Maggie. And it's not just because you're unavailable. It's something I can't even explain."

"Nick—"

"Please, just let me finish."

She waited.

"I know it's only been a week, but I can assure you, I'm not impulsive when it comes to love. Sex, yes, but not love. I've never felt this way before. And I've certainly never told a woman I loved her before."

It sounded like a line, but she knew from his eyes that it was true. She opened her mouth to speak, but he raised a hand to stop her.

"I don't expect anything I say to compromise your marriage. But I didn't want you to leave without knowing, just in case it did make a difference. And I guess even if it doesn't, I still want you to know that I…that I am madly, deeply, hopelessly, head over heels in love with you, Maggie O'Dell."

"It does make a difference, Nick," she said.

He seemed relieved by that simple revelation, as though it was more than he had ever hoped for.

"You know," he said, "you've helped me see a lot of things about myself, about life. I've been following in these huge, deep footsteps my father keeps leaving behind and…and I don't want to do that anymore."

"You're a good sheriff, Nick."

"Thanks, but it's not what I want," he continued. "I admire how much your job means to you. Your dedication—your stubborn dedication, I might add. I never realized before how much I want something like that, something to believe in."

"So what does Nick Morrelli want to be when he grows up?" she asked, smiling.

"When I was in law school I worked at the Suffolk County district attorney's office in Boston. They always said I was welcome to come back. I think I might give them a call."

"That sounds great," she said, already calculating the miles between Quantico and Boston.

"I'm going to miss you," he said simply. He checked his watch. "I should get you to the airport."

"Right." She closed down the computer, unplugging cords, snapping the lid shut and shoving it into its case. He grabbed her suitcase. She grabbed her garment bag. They were at the door when the phone rang. She hurried back and picked up the receiver.

"Maggie O'Dell."

"O'Dell, I'm glad I caught you."

It was Director Cunningham. She hadn't talked to him in days. "I was just on my way out."

"Good. Get back here as quickly as possible. I'm having Delaney and Turner meet you at the airport."

"What's going on?"

"I wanted you to know before you hear it on the news."

"Hear what?"

"Albert Stucky has escaped. They were transferring him from Miami to a maximum-security facility in North Florida. Stucky ended up biting the ear off one guard and stabbing the other with—get this—a wooden crucifix. Then he blew both their heads off with their own revolvers. Seems the day before, a Catholic priest visited Stucky in his cell. He had to be the one who left the crucifix. I don't want you to worry, Maggie. We got the bastard before, we'll get him again."

But the only thing Maggie heard was, "Albert Stucky has escaped."

One week later
Chiuchin, Chile

He couldn't believe how glorious the sun felt. His bare feet maneuvered the rocky shore. The minor cuts and scrapes were a small price to pay for the feel of the warm waves lapping at his feet. The Pacific Ocean stretched forever, its water rejuvenating, its power overwhelming.

Behind him, the mountains of Chile isolated this paradise, where poor, struggling farmers were as starved for attention as they were for salvation. The tiny parish included fewer than fifty families. It was perfect. Since he'd arrived, he hardly noticed the throbbing in his head. Perhaps it was gone for good this time.

A group of brown-skinned boys, clad only in shorts, chased a ball while they raced toward him. Two of them recognized him from the morning's mass. They waved and called out to him. He laughed at their mispronunciation of his name. When they gathered around him, he petted their black hair and smiled down at them. The one with the torn blue shorts had such sad eyes, reminding him of himself.

"My name," he instructed, "is Father Keller. Not Father Killer."

ACKNOWLEDGMENTS

I owe my deepest gratitude and appreciation to all those whose support and expertise made this fantastic journey possible.

Special thanks to:

Philip Spitzer, my agent, who enthusiastically offered to represent this book, then made it his personal mission to see it published. Philip, you are my hero.

Patricia Sierra, fellow author, for generously sharing her wisdom, her wit and her friendship.

Amy Moore-Benson, my editor, for her tenacity, her keen insights and her ability to make the editing process painless and rewarding.

Dianne Moggy and all the professionals at MIRA Books for their efforts and resolve to make this book a success.

Ellen Jacobs for always saying the right thing at just the right time.

Sharon Car, my writing cohort, for all those lunches commiserating with and encouraging me.

LaDonna Tworek, who helped me keep my perspective and encouraged me early on to hang in there.

Jeanie Shoemaker Mezger and John Mezger, who listened over all those free, delicious dinners they fed me.

Bob Kava for patiently answering all my questions about firearms.

Mac Payne, who gave me something to prove.

My parents, Edward and Patricia Kava, especially my mom for lighting all those candles of hope.

Writing, for the most part, is a solitary act, but it certainly wouldn't be possible for me without the loving support of my family and friends. Thanks also must go to Patti El-Kachouti, Marlene Haney, Nicole Keller, Kenny and Connie Kava, Natalie Cummings, Sandy Rockwood and Margaret Shoemaker.

Finally, thanks to Bob Shoemaker. This wouldn't have been the type of book Bob would even have read, but that would not have stopped him from being proud of me and telling everyone he met about it.

0908/BSC/APE

SERIAL KILLER RONALD JEFFREYS WAS EXECUTED FOR THREE MURDERS

Three months after his death, the body of a boy is found, killed in the same style as Jeffreys' victims.

Together, FBI profiler Maggie O'Dell and Sheriff Nick Morrelli start to uncover the gruesome picture of a killer – who has already been executed for his crimes.

Was Jeffreys convicted of crimes he didn't commit? Or has a cold-blooded killer been given the chance to perfect his crime?

OUT NOW

www.blackstarcrime.co.uk